ALL SIZED UP

"What do you think I am Mr. Gunn? Some lily-white sister of mercy raised in a convent?" Esmerelda was doing her best to impress Gunn with her sophisticated ways.

Gunn backed away, held up his hands in mock surrender. He liked Esmerelda's spunck, the way her eyes flashed with anger, and the rosiness that fury brought to her cheeks.

Esmerelda's anger subsided, and she smiled. "It's just that I don't think you should be sleeping on the floor when my bed's big enough—for two," she suggested, murmuring her last two words. There was a low husk in her voice, and her breasts pushed against the bodice of her gown, mounded above the cloth like ripening melons. The light danced on her skin, struck diamonds in her eyes.

Gunn focused on the outlines of her thighs underneath the thin cloth of her gown, and nodded toward the bed, "Are you sure it's big enough, Esmerelda?"

"Yes," she whispered, her eyes roaming his physique. "It'll do just fine."

#13

ARIZONA HARDCASE

GUNN

BY JORY SHERMAN

ZEBRA BOOKS
KENSINGTON PUBLISHING CORP.

ZEBRA BOOKS

are published by

KENSINGTON PUBLISHING CORP.
475 Park Avenue South
New York, N.Y. 10016

Printed in the United States of America

For Liselle,
who puts it all
together, somehow.
Unsung, maybe. Well,
I sing to her though
my clock runs slow.

CHAPTER ONE

It was tough as hell working alone.

Gunn snubbed the lariat around the corral post, walked along the taut rope to the blaze-faced bronco, bridle held behind his leg. The wild horse backed up, tightening the lariat even more, choking itself.

"Steady, boy," said Gunn. "Ease up." The horse glared at him with wide wild eyes. Gunn read the fear there, and the hatred. He brought the bridle up and the horse backed up gingerly.

As long as he kept the horse between him and the post, he was all right. If the blaze-face bolted, he'd have to start all over again.

He slipped the bridle over the horse's ears and face, buckled it around its neck.

This was the sixth horse he'd handled in the corral that morning. And the meanest. The worst was yet to come, he knew, even as he adjusted the bridle. The horse's eyes widened, its tongue thickened between sharp glaring teeth.

Gunn eased the horse toward him by pulling on the bridle reins. He slipped a hand under the lariat to loosen it.

The blaze-face's teeth dove at Gunn's arm.

He moved his arm, but not before sharp teeth grazed his flesh. Slobber soaked through the chambray material of his sleeve.

Gunn smiled, looked the horse straight in the eye.

"You got spirit, Blaze. All we got to do now is temper it some, see it's used right."

The horse snorted, white-eyed. Laid its ears back flat and bared its teeth.

Gunn dove in under the horse's neck just as its head struck like a rattlesnake's. He jerked the short rope from his pocket, hobbled the horse's forelegs before it realized what was happening. The tall man was out from under as the horse backed up, tightening the rope around its neck again.

"Go ahead, choke yourself to death, hoss," Gunn grinned. "But you and me are still going to tangle."

The horse stopped struggling against the rope, tried to shake off the bridle. This only made the rope tighten up more. The horse began pawing the ground with a forehoof. It fixed one baleful eye on the man walking across the corral through inch-thick dust.

Gunn bent over, picked up the saddle and blanket. He carried the saddle in his left hand, by the horn, the blanket in his right, rolled up tight. He walked within ten feet of the horse, dropped the saddle.

"Look at it good, boy," Gun told the young stud. He figured the horse to be at least two years old, no more than three. There were a few hide slashes that had healed over, which testified to the stallion's masculinity. Mares, or another stud, had marked him on the shoulders. The scars were like a soldier's chevrons, a badge of rank in the herd.

The horse backed away from him, keeping one stark eye on the saddle. Gunn grabbed up the reins with his left hand, shook out the blanket with the right. The sorrel with the blaze face spooked, spraddling his back legs as he tried to back away from the pressure on the bridle. Gunn went to his side, tossed the blanket. The horse snorted, dug in with its hind hooves. Gunn kept the blanket flowing over the horse's back, pulling it free, then tossing it back on.

Finally, the horse steadied, and Gunn set the blanket square, left it. He dropped the reins, picked up the saddle. Walking slowly toward the horse, he grabbed up the reins again as he drew up close. He held them loosely, brushed against the frightened animal as he spoke soothingly to him. He dropped the saddle gently, under the horse's belly, began rubbing the blanket down smooth. In a series of smooth motions, Gunn pulled on the reins, bowing the horse's neck. Then, he grabbed the saddle horn, swung it quickly onto the sorrel's back.

He kept the reins taut, pulling the horse's muzzle snug against its chest. With his free hand, he hooked one stirrup over the saddle horn to get it out of the way. The horse was backed against the corral fence, its head tucked back, neck bowed so that it could not jump out from under the saddle. Gunn ducked under the horse's belly, grabbed a cinch strap. He ran the strap through the front rigging ring. At the tightening of the cinch, the horse began to hump, bucking up against the saddle. Gunn made his loop and snugged up the cinch. He did the same with the rear strap, cinching up through the rear rigging ring.

Then he dropped the stirrup.

The horse kept bucking, stiffening up its forelegs. It tried to kick Gunn, but the cowman danced away.

"All right, old salt," he said, panting from the effort of saddling the wild bronc, "let's you and me get to it."

Gunn brought the reins up over the horse's head, held them with his left hand. He grabbed the saddle horn, hung on as the horse bucked and sidled away from him. He drew the reins in tight, waited for the right moment, then kicked a boot into the stirrup, swung up into the saddle.

The sorrel did it all, then, still hampered by the hobble. With bowed back, he kicked and hobbled forward.

Gunn lost his concentration when something caught the corner of his eye. An image, a spiral of dust hanging in the air.

That was enough for the blaze faced sorrel.

With a mighty leap, the horse bucked high, came down hard on stiffened forelegs. Gunn was jarred, jolted out of the saddle.

The sky spun crazily as with a sickening lurch, Gunn flew toward the ground. He landed with a bone-rattling thud. His eyes closed as his brain filled with black ink. Something cracked somewhere in his skull. The ground teetered as he tried to grab the earth itself and hold on.

His nose scuffed the dirt. His nostrils drew in snifters of the same dirt. Gunn sneezed and lights flashed behind his eyes.

He rolled away from the horse, which was lashing out with both hind hooves, whip-lashing the air with the sound of its grunting effort to lay Gunn out permanently.

Gunn stood up, swaying. He was out of wind, but he was not hurt. That cracking sound in his head had been only the sound of his neck bones being rearranged. His spine felt as if it had been snapped together and then stretched on a medieval rack.

"Sonofabitch!" Gunn cursed. Not at the horse, but at himself, for letting the animal throw him. He could have broken a leg or busted a kidney, he thought. Instead, he was covered with dust and the horse stood there now, a winner. Eyeing him like a bull about to charge.

The blaze face snorted, lowered its head.

Gunn walked away, climbed the fence. To get his breath, to look at the speck he had seen just before being tossed from the saddle.

He recognized the man riding toward the ranch along the road that led to Tucson.

T. O. Lassiter.

Owner of the Lazy L, where Gunn was breaking horses. Or, where a horse was breaking him.

The memory rose up in Gunn's mind.

A month ago he had ridden up, nursing Chico, who had gone lame. T. O. Lassiter had looked at Chico and shook his head.

"You won't ride that 'un again," he said.

"Not for a while," Gunn admitted.

"Likely not ever. That's cracked bone under that twitching hide." Gunn felt as carefully as had Lassiter and knew the man was right.

"Sell me a horse for cash?"

Lassiter shook his head.

"None to sell. Make you an offer though. Lots of wild horses in the hills. Good stock. You catch and break me a string for thirty days and you got the pick of the herd."

"Well, that's the goddamndest offer I ever heard."

Spitting into the dirt, Lassiter, a man so thin he scarce threw a shadow, had fixed Gunn with a single twinkling eye.

"It's the onliest one you're likely to get out here. You can walk on them boots heels till they're bald and your legs is cracked like that sorry mount of yours. Or you can hire on here for a month, with found, and get yourself a hundert dollar horse with legs born and bred in this god-forsaken country."

"I reckon I could catch up a horse solo, break him and ride on out after a day's work."

"Hah!" cackled Lassiter. "Try it, son! They's sidewinders and Gilas and prickly pears and *cholla* out there just waitin' fer a tenderfoot like you to walk right in amongst 'em! Try it!"

Gunn had seen the sense in Lassiter's words. Now, a month later, he was fit and lean as a whip, with some fine horseflesh broke to saddle. And a big black he had chosen for himself, sixteen hands high. Named him, too, a good name befitting his elegance and beauty. Esquire. Sound of limb, deep chested, with a sleek hide that shone in the sun like a crow's wing.

The month was up today and Lassiter had gone into Tucson to take care of last minute business as long as he had Gunn to watch his ranch. It wasn't much of a ranch, but Gunn had grown to respect it and its owner. T. O. was hard as a gnarled scrub cedar that grew from a craggy butte, but inside he was a tender-hearted man who lived his own way, out of touch with much of civilization. Not a bad way to live, Gunn thought, but Lassiter had not many years left if he worked his small spread alone. The land soaked the starch out of a man pretty quick in this land of blistering summers and bitter cold winters.

Lassiter rode up as Gunn picked himself up out of the dirt, stalked the victorious mustang.

"Thowed ye, eh?"

"Once," said Gunn.

Lassiter sat his horse, cackled with glee.

"He looks like he's got a couple more in him."

"Wanta bet?"

"A dollar says he puts you down again. Or rubs you off against a post."

"Done."

The slim man on horseback chuckled to himself, twirled an outsized handlebar moustache. Were it not for the moustache he would have looked like a youth from the front as well as from the other directions. Gunn knew his size was deceptive, though. Lassiter was as tough as an old boot. The only wrinkles on his face were around the eyes and lips. Probably because he laughed so much, enjoyed life better than most men knew how.

Gunn went toward the bronc on an angle. Indian-style, giving the horse no advantage. He drew his knife with a slick single motion, came up on the horse's blind side. Grabbed the reins with his left hand, jerked them hard. The horse's head came down and the animal began backing away, swinging its head to nip at Gunn.

"Fun's over, hoss."

Gunn slashed the hobbles, sheathed the knife quickly.

The horse started to balk, sidle away. Gunn kept the reins in his left hand. Then he reached up, grasped the horse's left ear. His fingers tightened firm on the ear. He twisted, hard, pushed down. The horse was distracted long enough for Gunn to swing up into the saddle, rein in hand. The bit braced against the horse's mouth.

"Toss me a quirt, T.O.!" Gunn called, as the sorrel began to fish-tail and twist, jumping straight up, coming down on all fours, stiff-legged. The jolts cracked Gunn's spine, sent ripples of pain up from his tail bone to his skull.

Lassiter unfurled his own quirt, waited until Gunn was in a certain position, tossed it to him. Gunn caught it deftly by the braided butt. The three-tassled horsewhip became a tool to teach the bucking bronco something about punishment for its behavior. Every time the horse bucked, Gunn lashed its rump. Hard.

Lassiter watched as Gunn gradually brought the horse under his domination. The animal finally tired. Gunn rode over to the corral fence, grabbed a rain slicker, began flapping that. The horse spun and stiff-legged it across the corral, but it didn't buck as before. Gunn made the slicker do tricks as he flapped it from side to side, over the horse's eyes. Until the animal got used to the noise and movement.

When the horse stood perfectly still, Gunn dismounted, stripped it from its saddle, turned the animal into another corral and pulled off its bridle.

Sweat and dust grimed Gunn's weathered face. His lips curled to a sensual smile as he walked towards Lassiter, holding out an empty palm. Lassiter dug, came up with a tattered five-dollar bill as Gunn climbed through the fence.

"Well, you broke the sumbitch."

Gunn took the five, stuffed it in his pocket. His slate gray eyes lit with pleasure. He liked Lassiter. It was going to be tough to leave him, but he'd written to Randall over a month ago, told him to meet him in Tucson. Jed ought to be there about now. Randall was a friend, one of the few close ones he had, who rode with him now and again.

"Thanks, T. O."

"Wash up and come inside. Got something to jaw with you about."

With that, Lassiter turned his horse, rode up to the small ranch cabin and beyond where he'd strip his horse, curry him down, fork him a hay biscuit.

Gunn's chambray shirt hung on him, drenched. Large sweat circles decorated the arm pits. His chaps flapped as he walked to the pump and a watering trough. He peeled his shirt off, rammed the pump handle up and down until water began to gush from its mouth. He sloshed off, unbuckled his chaps. His muscles ached with a good ache. His broad chest dried quickly in the dry air. His dark thick hair dripped over his broad shoulders. Gunn was tall, a shade over six feet, and he cast a shadow on the porch as his boots thudded against sound boards. Lassiter had built the cabin well. It boasted three bedrooms, a big living and eating room combination. The kitchen was small because Lassiter liked everything neat. Gunn went inside.

Lassiter handed him a glass of straight whiskey.

Gunn downed it, handed the glass back to Lassiter.

"I'll get a shirt, be back for a chaser."

A few moments later, Lassiter pulled a chair from the dining table, kicked it toward Gunn. The rancher was already sitting, a new bottle of whiskey in front of him, his glass half full. His eyes swam with water, narrowed as Gunn sat down, poured himself another three fingers of whiskey.

"You wanted for anything, Gunn?"

"Nope."

"Someone asking in town for you. Looked like a bounty hunter. Mean-eyed, carrying too much hardware for a peaceable man."

Gunn shrugged.

"The man have a name?"

"Name of Coker."

"Coker?" Gunn's face wrinkled up in thought. His pale gray eyes flickered.

"Yep. That was his handle. Mighty persistent cuss you ask me. Had a drink with him in Pima Flat. That's where he is, not in Tucson. I stood there on the way back, talked to the stage outfit there. He had come from Tucson."

"He just come out and ask?"

Lassiter eyed Gunn closely.

"Not right out. Didn't seem to know what you looked like. Described you as a big man. Said he lost you between Las Cruces and Tucson. To hear him tell it, he tracked you out of El Paso way."

"Then lost me between there and Tucson." Gunn grinned.

"You know him?" This Coker?"

"Maybe. Man about my age? Big, beefy."

"No. This 'uns right slender. No more'n in his early twenties."

Gunn's eyes closed for a minute. He thought of Laurie, his wife, how she had died back in '73. Up in Colorado on the Cache de la Poudre. But Jason Coker was responsible for that. If he hadn't raped her . . . he and his men . . . but Coker was in prison, anyway. Did he had a son? A brother? Maybe. Gunn didn't know.

"I wouldn't worry about it, T. O. A kid like that. He'll get bored, ride on."

"Not this one. Besides, he ain't alone."

Gunn eyebrows went up like flags.

"He's got five hardcases with him, and they're all dry behind the ears."

CHAPTER TWO

Gunn finished his second drink, reached for the makings. He stretched his legs out, rolled a quirlie. Outside, a horse nickered.

Lassiter stared at Gunn, his eyes full of more questions.

Gunn stuck the cigarette in his mouth, struck a sulphur match.

He had questions of his own.

Memories.

He couldn't shut them out. Couldn't ignore Coker. A man persistent as that wouldn't just ride on. Lassiter had said he was a young man. So he couldn't be Jason Coker, the man responsible for his wife's murder. A relative, perhaps. A son. A brother.

"How in hell did this Coker track me to Pima Flat?"

Lassiter shrugged.

"Anyone else know you'd be out this way?"

"Feller back in El Paso. Jed Randall."

"That's it, then," said Lassiter.

"Huh?" Gunn blew a plume of smoke in the air.

The burning tobacco raked his throat, scratched his lungs.

"Randall's in Pima Flat. Asking the same questions. Went to Tucson, same as Coker. No sign of you there, so he backtracked."

"You tell 'em I was out here?"

"Nope. Figger that's your business."

Gunn grinned at T.O. Lassiter had grown on him in the past month. He liked the old man's grit and determination.

"That ain't all, o' course."

"I gathered that, T.O. You're about as hard to pry as a mussel on a rock."

"Yep. That's so."

Lassiter, Gunn could see, was going to make him wait a while before he furnished any more information.

"My daughter's comin' in from Bowie on the afternoon stage. You'll like L.D."

"L.D. What kind of name is that for a woman?"

"Call her that, 'cause I been called T.O. all my born days. Her name's Esmerelda. I hate the name. An all-fired mouthful of mush. So does she. Her ma tagged her with that handle and we called her 'Merelda' until she growed up and asked everybody to call her L.D."

"What's the T.O. stand for?"

Lassiter grinned wide and flashed a wink.

"Theodosius Owensmouth."

Gunn muttered an oath, matched T.O.'s grin.

"No wonder you use your initials."

Lassiter got up from the table, favoring his creaking joints as he straightened up. Gunn could almost hear his bones creak.

"Want to spriten up the place afore L.D. gets here. She's been visitin' kin in Texas for nigh a year. Regular tomboy when she left here. I guess that's partly my doin's. Raised her like a boy and folks say she's a chip off the old block. I missed her powerful, but my sis and her husband wanted to see her and maybe teach her some refinement. Houston society folk!" T.O. snorted and picked up a feather duster in the corner. There was more dust on it than in the room. T.O. sneezed when he shook it.

"I'll remind you," said Gunn, getting up from the table, "my month's up today."

"You make it sound like a sentence in the hoosegow."

"Well . . ."

"You picked your horse yet?"

"That big sorrel out there. Sixteen hands high, with the four white stockings."

"Hmm," mused T.O., nearly knocking a vase from a table, "you got a good eye, son. Best of the bunch."

"I reckon."

"What you gonna call him?"

"Esquire."

"Right smart name."

"Suits him," said Gunn, walking toward his room in the back. L.D.'s room, he guessed. Some of her things were still there. Not much sign of a girl, though. More like a boy's room. He began packing his few belongings, loading up his saddle bags.

Lassiter looked in on him almost an hour later. Gunn had heard him banging around the house, fetching fresh water, sweeping out the kitchen.

"You ain't aimin' to go into Pima Flat, are you?" Lassiter asked.

"Randall's waiting for me there, you said."

"You got six men gunning for you, son. You go on to Tucson. I'll get word to your friend where to look you up."

"No need. Have to face them sooner or later anyway. Coker's got a wild hair up his ass. If he's related to Jason Coker."

"Bad blood between you two, eh?"

"There was. It happened a long time ago. When I had a wife, a ranch."

"She dead? Your woman?"

"Yes. She's dead, T.O."

"Coker kill her?"

"No. He just raped her. Someone else murdered her."

Gunn's jaw hardened and there was a mist in his pale eyes as he remembered Laurie. Coker and his bunch came to the ranch when he was gone, put the boots to Laurie. Beat her up pretty badly. Hurt her. Inside. There wasn't much left of her memory now. Certain poses he recalled. Her smile. Her eyes. The way she walked. And, now that the memories had been dredged off, that awful moment when he had come back to the ranch and discovered her. Looked into her eyes and saw the pain, the haunted look that comes just before death. The *knowing* look. Like an animal shot mortally. He couldn't forget that look. He had seen it then and he had seen it since.

Her body, that temple he had worshiped inside, that sleek flesh had been bruised, torn, ravaged. He couldn't forget that either. Men had come and beaten her, violated her during her last hours of life. He couldn't forget that. He had learned the dark side of men and he had seen enough of that darkness to last him a long time. Perhaps such sights shortened his patience. Made him a mite too quick on the trigger, the draw. Or maybe he wanted to see good, but couldn't anymore. Except in men like T.O., Randall. A few others. And in a few women. He didn't want to be bitter. But Laurie's death had changed him. Tempered something inside him he didn't understand. Drawn out a violence in him that he would rather keep hidden. Yet he had faced it. He had killed. Each time, a sadness like a curtain would cloak him and he'd want to ride on, toward the sunset, hoping to find a place where people lived in peace. He had ridden far. He had seen some good things and some bad. The land was still restless, untamed, but it was not the land that made men bad. It was something in their natures, their hearts. And the badness was a horror. A horror that could ravage a woman like Laurie and leave her to die.

"I'm awful sorry, Gunn."

Gunn turned to face T.O. He did not wipe his eyes. The tears glistened there, like dew on soft blue stones.

"Every godamned person in the world should be sorry for such a thing," he said.

T.O. shuddered. His head dropped and he left the room. His face flushed as if exposed to a blast furnace.

The hoofbeats sounded on the hard ground.

Gunn heard them, quickened.

He heard T.O.'s boots bang hollow on the boards of the house as he went to the front door.

Gunn's right hand curled around his holster. He clasped the grip on his pistol. An unconscious thing. It had been peaceful here. For a month. Now, things were changing. Things were happening fast. It was time to move on, but maybe he had waited a day too long.

She was a beauty.

He saw her from the front window. Saw part of T.O.'s shoulder and arm as the rancher stood on the porch. The woman was young, her face shadowed by the hat she wore. She wasn't riding side-saddle; her skirt was bunched up in the saddle and she didn't flop on it like a sack of potatoes.

The man riding alongside her was another matter. His hat was riding on his shoulder, a thong tugging at the Adam's apple on his throat. He wore his pistol tied low on his leg, his gunbelt bristled with new cartridges. His hair was neatly trimmed, his clothes fresh brushed. He had thin lips, a weak chin. Gunn took him to be in his early twenties, despite his deep-sunk eyes that gave his face a gaunt, haunted look.

He had seen many of his kind. All along the border, up in Kansas, Abilene, Dodge, beyond the forts in the gold country. Young gun toughs. Glaze-eyed, wild, cocky as roosters. Spoiling for a fight, or ready to jump the first woman who looked bat-eyed at them. This one was no different. Maybe a little less seedy than some of them, but the cant was the same—slightly off-tilt. Like a cast in the eye, or a twitch, such men gave themselves away. This one wore the low-slung pistol, the thonged hat, the tight trousers, delicate, fidgety hands, empty face, eyes vacant as a doll's. As the couple rode closer, Gunn looked at the youth's eyes more closely. There was something vaguely familiar about them.

The girl spoke first and Gunn had his answer.

"Hello, Pa. Mister Coker here was kind enough to offer me assistance," she cooed, affecting a sophistication that did not suit her well. "He's just the nicest man and all. Rode out here with me so that I wouldn't be captured by wild Indians or eaten by wolves."

"Few Indians out here and the wolves have been trapped out," said T.O. wryly. "But set down, Mister Coker and I thank you fer bringin' my daughter out."

"The name's Randy Coker, Mister Lassiter," said the youth, an edge of arrogance in his tone. "L.D. is sure a nice lady. Your daughter, I mean, sir."

"Randy, this is my father, T.O., and . . ." her eyes fixed on Gunn's, eyelashes dipping coyly . . . "why I don't believe I know this gentleman."

"T.O. started to open his mouth, but Gunn spoke up quickly.

"Smith," he said. "Jason Smith."

Gunn watched Randy's eyes carefully as the man swung out of the saddle. He did some things right. Didn't turn his back on anyone there. Randy helped L.D. off her horse and then stepped up to face T.O. and Gunn.

"My pa's named Jason," said young Coker. "Not a common name."

Gunn was silent.

The girl looked at the two men, cocked her head. An odd light came into her eyes.

"Randy's pa broke out of jail," she said.

T.O. grunted, not looking at Gunn. It was as if he sensed something building, a fire maybe.

"Well, not out of jail," said Randy. "They led him into the Denver Courthouse for an appeal. That was three months ago. I knew he wouldn't get no fair hearing. Soon as they had taken the cuffs off, me and my friends threw down on the bailiff and we took off. Pa caught a bullet, but he's mendin' just fine."

"What's your pa supposed to have done?" Gunn asked evenly. He was calm, but his palms had started to sweat.

"Nothin'. Falsely accused by a no-account skunk name of Gunnison. Calls himself Gunn now. Usin' an alias like the coward he is. No matter. I'm lookin' for him and when I find him, I'll shoot him down like the dog he is."

T.O. coughed, looked down at his feet.

His daughter let out a brief sigh.

Gunn looked into Randy's eyes, seeing the hate there, feeling it like a torch across his own face. His gray-blue eyes went cloudy, but his face showed no outward sign of the churning inside him. For a moment he was tempted to draw his pistol and shoot the youth down in his tracks. Kill him quick before he could do any harm. Instead, he smiled without showing his teeth.

"Come inside, have a drink," suggested T.O. "Hitch your horses to the rail. We can put 'em up later."

"Mighty nice of you, Mister Lassiter," said Randy, his innocence no less galling to Gunn than his youthful arrogance. For a moment, though, he had been close to death. The son was not guilty of his father's crimes, but somehow Gunn sensed the same evil in Randy that flowed through Jason's veins. A bad seed blooming again, needing to be snuffed out, stamped out, crushed, buried—forever.

Inside, Randy continued his narrative, a fabrication handed down to him by his father, concerning Jason's innocence, Gunn's guilt. His tongue loosened by whiskey, he rambled on about scenes he had not witnessed, people he had not known.

"This Gunnison is a pure killer. Ice water in his veins. He killed a dozen men up on the Poudre and a woman or two."

Gunn winced inwardly.

"Women?" piped L.D. "He must be an awful man!"

T.O. growled low in his throat, condemned to silence by his brief friendship with the man who sat at his table.

"Oh, he's a snake, that one," said Randy. "But I really shouldn't talk anymore of such a scoundrel in front of Miss Lassiter."

Gunn's attention shifted to the young woman. T.O.'s daughter. With her bonnet off, he saw that she had soft blonde hair. Her eyes were blue as cornflowers. She resembled her father only superficially. Her high forehead, prominent cheekbones, small square chin showed the lines of that side of the family. Her eyes and mouth must have been inherited from her mother. She was beautiful, trim of figure, curves in the right places. Young, she couldn't have been more than twenty, and she had a healthy glow in her cheeks that emphasized her age. It was obvious to Gunn that she was much taken with the wild young man whose cheeks were flushed from drink. She looked at Randy with frank admiration, treated him with interest and cordiality.

T.O. saw where matters were headed and he corked the whiskey bottle, withdrew it just as Randy reached out a hand.

"Better put this away 'fore we all get in trouble," T.O. said.

Randy pouted.

L.D.'s face clouded as she looked at her father.

"Pa, our guest might like another."

"Time for our guest to head on back into town, Esmerelda. This here's a workin' ranch and we've sat around, jawed enough."

"Well!" exclaimed his daughter. "I no more'n get back and you . . ."

Randy stood up, scraping his chair. He reached for his hat, grasped its brim and tipped it.

"Your Pa's right. Time I got back into town, see to my pa, things. That Gunn feller might show up anytime. Right, mister?"

Gunn's eyes flickered.

"Right, Randy. You wouldn't want to miss him."

"Uh, no."

Esmerelda fumed while Randy untied his horse, mounted up. He turned and waved, frowned when he saw Gunn standing next to her.

After Coker rode out of sight, L.D. turned on her father.

"You were quite rude to Mister Coker, Pa! You treated him like some kind of bug. He was nice enough to ride out here with me. The buckboard's broken and I couldn't bring my baggage. I was going to wait until tomorrow to come out, but Randy—Mister Coker—was kind enough to accompany me. Just so's I could see you again, Pa."

T.O. bowed his head, accepting her verbal abuse.

Gunn saw T.O.'s head drop in resigned silence and a nerve jangled, an alarm sounded in his brain.

"You're the rude one, ma'am, talkin' to your pa like that. You showed no respect for either your father or custom by bringing trash like that out to his home. Your home."

"Trash? How dare you call him trash? Why, you're nothing but a saddle bum. I've seen your kind in Houston. Drifter. I'll bet your name isn't even Smith. Pa, what's this man doing here? I don't like him one bit!"

T.O. started to say something, but Gunn lifted his hand. It was his problem, not Lassiter's.

"No, ma'am. My name isn't 'Smith.' The name is Gunn and I'm the man who put Jason Coker in prison."

Esmerelda reacted as if Gunn had slapped her. She drew back, her eyes widened.

"You . . . you . . ."

"Hold on," said T.O. "We haven't heard Gunn's side of it yet. Maybe he'll tell us. Suddenly I'm down right curious myself!"

CHAPTER THREE

Jason Coker looked out the hotel window, licked his dry lips.

The years in prison had thinned him down, made him lean, given his a feral look. His hair had thinned more, too, and the steely gray on the sides had crept higher on his head. His eyes were rheumy, his flesh pale except for his windburned face. His deep barrel chest had begun to sink, to draw in from those years of confinement. His thick eyebrows still gave his face a craggy look and his nose still jutted over a neatly trimmed moustache, bulbed at his nostrils. His eyes were still chestnut hazel, the colors changing with the light. The thinness had not harmed his handsome features, but only enhanced them. His heavy frame no longer carried the bulk he once had, but at five foot ten, he still presented a formidable figure. He gripped a cigar the same old way, his hand sporting the ring with a ruby set in gold that he had worn in Colorado when he went to prison. He had hung on to the moustache, the ring, the craving for stogies with that same possessive sense that had driven him to push Gunn off the Cache la Poudre by raping his wife, framing Gunn himself for murder.

Coker had seen his dreams ground into dust by Gunn. Born into an impoverished New York family, the blood of Scots, Irish and Welsh in his veins, Coker had run away from home at the age of fourteen. He had traveled to Missouri, drifted over into Kansas where he began working cattle until the war between the States broke out. He had fought on the North's side, then discovered, as so many others had, that Texas held the promise of riches. Texas was big, open, and there were wild cattle to be picked up by an enterprising man who could sit a saddle and work a cow horse. Dissatisfied with working the brush for strays, Coker soon learned a few shortcuts: he hired hard men adept with the running iron and built a herd more quickly than before. With half a dozen brands registered, he kept the running irons hot and sent or drove herds up the Shawnee and Chisholm Trails. These drives were so successful that Coker was able to put away the running iron and earn his living from cattle in an easier way. He bought low and sold high. When the Goodnight-Loving Trail opened, Coker knew he could cut his losses and make even more money. It was risky going through the Indian Territory into Kansas, where skinflint buyers took advantage of men who had to sell or starve. The Chicago beef market was a different story. There, Coker could drive a hard bargain and get his prices. He became rich and soon attracted men to him who could provide an even more powerful lever in the market place. By forming a cattle cartel, Coker could dictate prices at the Chicago stockyards and freeze out competition.

Even Gunn was attracted to Coker in the beginning. Coker was a success. No one knew anything of his background. Indeed, such backgrounds were commonplace and it was a rare man who was not acquainted with the running iron. Gunn's ranch on the Poudre thrived because Coker led the way. He showed Gunn and the other ranchers in northwest Colorado how to make money and he made money along with them.

And then, in a single winter and a searing summer, the tides of fortune had shifted. Coker, a greedy, possessive man, had dreams of building an empire, but he had made one mistake. He knew cattle and he knew the marketplace, but he had yet to learn how to read land. His own ranch location turned out to be a costly misjudgment. His own cattle suffered when the river changed course. His stock ponds dried up in the drought and the ranchers to the south of him crowded him away from the Platte.

It was then that he had gone after Gunn's ranch on the Poudre. It was another costly mistake.

Now he meant for Gunn to pay.

He watched his son ride up the street, not hurrying. Randy was a good son. A little cocky and quick to anger, but he could be tempered in time.

Jason limped away from the window, favoring his left leg. The ball had gone clean through, but the flesh was not yet fully healed. The bone was bruised. He had been lucky. A few inches higher and he'd either be talking in a high-pitched voice or be minus a dozen yards of gut.

He sat at the table, poured himself a drink from the bottle of whiskey he had opened a short while before. He fished in his vest for a cigar, stuck it in his mouth without lighting it. He wet the end, took the cigar out and drank half the shotglass of whiskey. His eyes filled with tears. He lit the cigar while his eyes cleared and adjusted his weight on the chair. Waiting was hard now. No sign of Gunnison and his son getting too well known in town. Chasing off with that young girl when he should have been close by in case Gunnison showed up. Only it wasn't Gunnison anymore. Captain Gunnison in the War. He called himself just Gunn and his name was already a legend.

Gunn had beaten him once. He would not live long enough to do so again. Something had happened up in that valley. Something had hardened the man called Gunn so that he was not the easy mark Jason had taken him for in the beginning. No one thought a lone man could stand against Coker's outfit. Yet Gunn had wiped them all out, brought him down. The memory was still a bitter taste in Coker's mouth. Prison had made him reflective, hardened him as well. And his son was standing by him now, full-grown, quick with a pistol, a sure shot with rifle.

Things had gotten out of hand that day he had visited the Gunnison ranch. They had meant to lay the blame on Gunnison for raping and beating his own wife, but Fate had taken a hand. Gunnison had eluded the trap set for him and gone on a killing rampage; tracking down Coker's men one by one, and finally, trapping Coker himself.

His situation now was not good. Jason knew that. He was a fugitive, fair game for bounty hunters. Randy, for all his growing up, was quick-tempered, what some would call a hothead, and, what others would call a hardcase. The boy wouldn't listen to reason. He didn't realize how dangerous Gunn had become. Still, Randy had quickness on his side. He might be a match for a man like Gunn. If the odds were stacked in his favor. The men with him could provide the needed edge. They were experienced, rough, killers. If Gunn was still riding a lone trail and had no idea that Jason had broken out of prison, he could be taken. Quick. Easy.

The knock on the door came as Jason sipped the rest of the whiskey in the shot glass.

"Randy?"

"Yeah. I'm back."

"Door's open."

Randy came in, wearing a wide grin. Swaggering. Jason looked up at his son, frowned.

"Sit down," said his father, a gruff edge to his voice.

"Sure, Pa. Hell, you don't mind me goin' off like that. With a purty gal. It's so damn quiet here I was getting bored."

"This isn't a game, Randy. We're not here for fun."

"Awww . . ." Randy reached for the bottle, but his father grabbed it away from him.

"You talk first," Jason said. "Stranger in town. Lassiter was talkin' to him down in the saloon."

"Yeah, I know. Randall. Out of El Paso."

"Maybe. He's waitin' for someone. Backtracked here same as us. Gunn was in El Paso, too."

"You think Randall's waitin' for Gunn, Pa?"

"Might be." Jason poured himself another drink.

Randy's eyes got hard as flints and he licked his lips. "We get finished here, you go down and talk with him. Be polite. Listen."

"Aw Pa . . ."

"Now you better tell me about Lassiter's daughter. Lassiter lit out of here quick after talking to that Randall jasper. Seems he might have waited around for the gal to get here and rode her out himself."

"I met her pa in town and he said he had to get back to the ranch. I figgered I'd ride his daughter out. Glad I did now. For a couple of reasons."

Jason's eyebrows lifted. He waited for his son to continue.

"Lassiter had a hired hand breakin' horses. Dumb jasper."

"He have a name?"

"Why, yeah, Pa," Randy grinned. "Same as yours. Jason."

"Jason?"

"Yeah. Jason Smith."

Coker snorted, looked at his son as if eyeing an imbecile.

"What'd he look like?"

"Tall, wide-shouldered. Dark hair, long as rope, thick."

Jason sat up rigid, his senses percolating like boiled water.

"His eyes, Son, what color were his eyes?"

Randy rolled his lower lip into his mouth, wet it while he thought.

"Why, they warn't no color at all."

"Huh? Say that again?"

"Pa. His eyes were real pale. Like a couple of dull nickels."

"Gray? Were they gray? Pale blue?"

"I reckon. Shit, what difference does it make?"

Jason Coker clenched his fists, slid them toward him on the table top. He looked at his son with fierce eyes, eyes flickering with recognition.

"That's him! Gunn! You dumb kid, you shook hands with the man I'm bound to kill!"

"No!"

"Yes, dammit. Who else could it be? We know he left El Paso. He didn't go to Tucson. His partner's down in the saloon waitin' for him and where is he? He's holed up out there at Lassiter's and you told him your name. He's no fool. He can put two and two together. If you weren't so ga-ga over that gal, you would have noticed it. I've told you what he looks like often enough."

Recognition softened Randy's face. His eyes glittered as he tried to picture the man he had met. It might have been Gunn, at that. Could have been.

"But the man said his name was . . ."

"Shit! Jason Smith? He was pullin' your damned leg, Randy!" Coker stood up, winced as he put weight on his game leg. "Jason Smith my ass. That was Gunn!"

"Yeah, Pa. I reckon. But hell, I didn't know."

"You should have. Tall man with pale eyes, eyes pale as pewter spoons. It's a wonder he didn't throw down on you right then. Damn! I wished I'd been there in your place!"

Randy stood up, stalked his father across the room. Jason stood by the window, the light ironing out his face until it was smooth with a deep hatred welling up inside him. He clutched the curtain with his right hand as if squeezing a man's neck.

"I—I'll go back out there, Pa. I'll get him. Me and the boys will . . ."

"No," said Jason quietly, turning to face his son. "You won't get him your way, Randy. Not now. He knows you. Knows your face. Likely old man Lassiter already told him you were in town. He just sat out there, foxy as could be and waited for you. Sized you up while you were mooning over Lassiter's daughter. No, that's not the way. He'll be ready for such a move. And Gunn's smart. I've told you that. Damned smart."

"Then, how . . ."

"Just wait a minute. Let me think. I tried it that way. I put the best men I had against him and he beat every one of them. Good men, as hard as they come. Gunn's fast. He's smart. You go at him head on and he'll beat you."

"Aw, shit. He's just a man. He didn't impress me much."

Jason looked at his son with pity. He shook his head, sighed deeply. Randy was tough. He had been on his own, gotten some temper, but he was still no match for Gunn. Not without favorable odds. Even in prison, the stories had reached Jason and he had listened to them carefully, separating the wheat from the chaff. Gunn had made a reputation for himself, up in Montana, in Colorado, Wyoming, south along the border. Men coming in to prison had seen him along the owl-hoot trail. Others had crossed his trail and had stories to tell of the man with the cold pale eyes.

"I tried it your way, Randy," said Jason slowly. "And I failed. Gunn won't be caught in a rabbit trap. Because he's not a rabbit. He doesn't run. He doesn't back down. But, he can't get caught in a fox trap either, because he isn't a fox."

"I—I don't understand."

"Gunn is dangerous because he does two things well. He thinks and he is not afraid to die. For another, he's a killer. Cold-blooded as any. I know. I've seen his work at close hand."

"I'm not afraid, either. And I could kill a man. I could kill Gunn."

Jason smiled indulgently at his son. He patted Randy on the shoulder.

"I know," said Jason. "Good. Don't be afraid of him. But don't underestimate him either. I've thought about him hard for these past years, these past three months. I've figgered him every way I can and I think he can be brought down. Not in a straight face-to-face shootout, maybe. But another way. Through cunning and knowing where he's weak."

"Hell, Pa, he looked like an ordinary hired hand. He didn't show me much. We sat there jawin' and he looked about as dangerous as a mule."

"Looks can be deceiving, Son. Listen to me."

Randy's eyes turned flinty with impatience.

"This Gunn has one big weakness, Randolph. He's tenderhearted. He loved his woman back then and it made him kind of crazy when she got killed. He made some mistakes, but we didn't get onto him until it was too late. The law should have put him prison instead of me. But it didn't work out that way. Even after his wife died, though, he didn't let up on the women. He likes them. Likes them a lot. So, I say we let him get close to another woman. Then go after her. That's the secret. He'll go plumb crazy. Then, you can take him. Easy."

"I thought you said this Gunn did you wrong. You act like you done him wrong. Pa?"

"He did, he did. I'm just saying you got to get him through a woman. Think about it."

Randy walked back to the chair, sat down. His eyes dulled as he thought about what his father had said.

"You ain't askin' me to let Gunn loose with the Lassiter gal? L.D.?"

"That her name? No. Just see to it that there are gals availabale when he comes into Pima Flat. Shouldn't be too hard."

"No. That Randall feller seems mightly familiar with the ladies at the saloon."

Jason's eyes lit up. He leaned on the cane, limped to the chair. He pushed the bottle across the table toward his son.

"That's your answer, Son. Randall will do the introductions. You keep an eye on him. Gunn will be along directly, find him a woman. If he's been out on that ranch for a time without no female companionship, he's bound to want to dip his wick."

"Yeah," said Randy, pouring a drink in a shot glass. "I'll get the boys to keep an eye on Randall. Gunn doesn't know any of 'em and I can just wait until the time is right. I'd love to plug the bastard while he's pumping one of those gals."

"That would be the time," said Jason, his disposition brightening for the first time that day. "I may even help you."

CHAPTER FOUR

Gunn was ready to leave.

T.O. had other ideas.

"Stay the night at least," he told Gunn. "My daughter and I want you to be our guest for supper."

"I don't think the lady wants me around, T.O. Best I get to it."

"You go into Pima Flat, they'll take you," said Lassiter, his voice pitched low. He and Gunn were on the porch, feeling alien in the house now that a woman had invaded it.

"I know," said Gunn, looking out at the horses. He was restless. Coker was in Pima Flat and no telling how he'd rigged the deck this time. The man was responsible for Laurie's death even though he hadn't pulled the trigger. He had set it up. He had raped her. And then turned his men loose on her like a pack of slavering dogs. Men like Coker were society's cancers and if the prisons couldn't hold such men then maybe six feet of ground could.

"Why go in then? You can stay here. Or ride on past, go to Tucson. I could get word to your friend Randall."

T.O. stepped off the porch, sat on a step. He picked up a strand of straw, stuck it in his mouth. Gunn sat beside him, suddenly weary.

"Look, T.O., you never asked and I didn't tell you. But Coker is one of those men whose insides are rotted out. The law couldn't keep him locked up and now he's loose. If I don't take him out, he's just big grief prowling the land. He didn't kill my wife, but he and his men raped her and left her to die. He's plumb bad stuff and I can't ride on by without so much as a 'by-your-leave.' "

Esmerelda started to come outside to join the men when she stopped, overhearing Gunn's words. She drew back, listening, not wanting to eavesdrop, but not able to help herself.

"You're a hard man, Gunn. And maybe you got a reason to be bitter. I don't know what makes you tick. But you got a place here. You did right by me and you handle horses well. The Lazy L will grow if you stay on. I'd consider it working out to a partnership deal. You can't just go on riding over every godamned hill and expect to stay alive. Man's got to settle down. How long ago you lose your wife? Two years, three?"

"Longer than that. Closer to five."

"Well, no wonder you're turning sour as pig's feet in brine. You're packing a hard load. 'Minds me of a story I heard once't 'bout a scout and a soldier got separated from their outfit during an Injun fight. They come upon the river, wantin' to cross and seed an Injun woman what escaped from the scrap. All bedraggled and forlorn, all she wanted to do was get crost that river and find a hold to hide in. Well, the scout, he took compassion on that woman, heisted her up on his pony and rode her on across, while the soldier, he grumbled to beat hell.

"On the other side, the scout he let the old woman down and she scrambled off on her own. The soldier, he bitched to high blue heaven for twenty mile and never said nothing right specific. Just wondered what in hell an Army scout was doing hauling an enemy woman crost a river 'stead of shootin' her dead and claimin' an Injun scalp.

"Well, the scout he pulled up directly and looked at that soldier and said calm as you please, 'hell, man, I helped an old woman cross a damned river. Looks to me like you're still a-carryin' her. I left her back there on the bank.' "

Gunn drew in a breath, cocked his boot up on its heel.

"Reckon you're right, T.O. I pack some baggage with me. Didn't think I did 'till I heard about Coker and saw his son ride up here. There's a way to shuck it, though."

"Eh? How so?"

"I'm going to kill Coker. Jason Coker. His son, too, if he gets in the way."

T.O. turned his head. Faced Gunn. There was a wetness in his eyes. A pain there. Trying to get out. Gunn looked at him hard and saw something back of the gaze. Something flickering on Lassiter's face. Something he had not seen before. Even as he looked, T.O. glanced away and Gunn saw another thing: the look of a man trying to come to grips with a terrible secret.

Lassiter's hands were palsied, trembling almost

imperceptibly. Gunn had seen it before, but not so pronounced. Now, Lassiter seemed to be about to rattle apart. The tremors in his hands spread to his arms, his shoulders, his chest and back. He shook until his clothes moved on his frame.

"What's wrong with you, T.O.?"

"I've a cancer."

"How long you known?"

"A couple of months."

"Bad?"

"The rope'll play out soon, haul me up short."

"Esmerelda know?"

"Nope. Just you. And if you tell her, I'll kill you."

"You put a hell of a load on a man."

"I'm not askin' you to stay a long time, Gunn. Just until . . ."

Gunn shook his head, stood up. He muttered an oath under his breath. He looked up, saw the face bob back through the doorway. Esmerelda hadn't been quick enough. She had heard everything.

T.O. sucked in a breath, brought his palsy under control. But there were beads of sweat in the furrows on his forehead. His face was drenched with perspiration.

"Hang on, T.O.," Gunn said. "I won't run out on you. But I've got to go into Pima Flat, take care of that Coker business."

"Yair. I reckon you do."

Gunn tried to help T.O. to his feet, but the old man shook off Gunn's hand. His pride was still strong, Gunn thought. But inside, Lassiter was rotting away, falling apart. It was a terrible thing to see.

A horrible way for a good man to die.

Jed Randall stood at the bar in the San Carlos Hotel sipping his whiskey. The girl he was was waiting for had not come downstairs yet and the afternoon was getting away from him.

Tom Yire, the bartender, shot a glance in his direction, hunched a shoulder in the direction of the lobby.

Jed turned so that he could look at the mirror, see who was coming into the saloon. He was a short man, six or seven inches under six feet, with straw hair, wrinkles at the corners of his brown eyes. His legs were bowed from years in the saddle. His face was weathered from sun and wind, smooth-shaven, taut as a drumhead.

Three men came through the doorway. Two of them, he knew slightly. Had met them a day or two before. Bat Hudson and Paul Burns. Hardcases. Scowl-eyed men with moustaches, sideburns, thick brows, as if poured into a common mold and ejected before either was tempered. Bat was short, thick-legged and thick-armed, with dark hair and eyes, bad teeth. Paul was slightly taller, leaner, and yet dark like his confrere. These two took a table, signalled to Yire for a bottle and glasses.

The other man strode toward Jed until his face appeared next to his in the mirror.

"Randall. I'm Randy Coker."

Jed turned, looked into the sallow face of the youth, peered into the flinty eyes as if trying to fathom what was going on upstairs in his brain.

"Yeah. I know."

"Buy you a drink?"

"I've got one. It'll do me."

"Some talk, then."

"You know the price of talk."

"I saw your friend. The one you're waiting for. Gunn."

Jed's senses prickled.

"I reckon I've mentioned his name a time or two."

"Yeah. He ought to be coming into town directly. Saw him at Lassiter's Lazy L. Had a drink with him."

Something was wrong, but Randall couldn't put his finger on it. The name Coker was familiar to him. Vaguely familiar. He had heard it before. But where?

"Well, I'll be waiting for him."

"Thought so. You and him good friends?"

Jed shifted his weight, stepped away from Coker as if to size him up in a different light. The man was prying now and Jed didn't like it. Coker had stepped over an invisible line. Such a thing could be dangerous. Jed looked at Hudson and Burns. Both men were watching him closely, scowling. Well, he was outgunned, no question about that. Coker was a snot-nosed kid and probably didn't know any better.

"We know each other."

"None of my business, but when you see Gunn, tell him I said howdy."

"I'll do that. But you just saw him. What, two hours ago?"

"About three. Didn't know he was your friend though. He used a different name."

Jed's eyebrows went up. He had met Lassiter, mentioned Gunn's name to him. Now this Coker feller was sticking his nose in. Maybe Lassiter had said something to Gunn about Coker and his bunch. What was going on? Why would Gunn use an alias? Was he afraid of this pipsqueak? Maybe he knew about the others. Jack Martin, Slicker Langley and Pete Cantwell. But there was another man with the bunch and no one had seen hide nor hair of him. Stayed up in his room. A cripple, someone had said.

"What do you want, Coker?"

"Nothing, Randall. Just trying to be friendly."

Jed tossed off his drinks, stiffened as it took hold, burned down his throat. Above the saloon floor, on the balcony, he saw her hesitate, then smile at him.

Willa Gleeson waved.

Jed waved back.

"Excuse me," he told Coker. "Here's the company I was expectin'."

Coker smiled wanly and moved back to the table. He said something to the two men. Money jingled on the tabletop and the three men left, taking the bottle with them.

Tom Yire came over.

"What was that all about, Jed?"

"Beats me," Randall shrugged. "You never know what comes out of the wood."

"I'd trust an Apache before I'd have truck with that bunch."

"Thanks for the advice," Jed grinned, as Wilda Gleeson walked toward him.

She moved past the tables, empty at this time of day, but teeming with talk and the snick of cards at night. She was a graceful woman in her early twenties, with her light brown hair tied back away from her heart-shaped face. Her hair hung to just past her shoulder blades. Her light summer frock scarcely concealed an hourglass figure, the hem short enough to reveal her trim ankles. Her blue eyes twinkled as she stepped into Jed's warm embrace.

"Took your time," he said.

"I wanted to look fresh for you. Did you have any trouble with those men?"

"Nope. Just jawed with that Coker kid a minute."

"Well, you be careful. I hear they're in town to kill a man."

"Where'd you hear that?"

"Around. Last night, with one of the men dancin'."

Willa worked for the hotel which owned the saloon. She didn't have to sell her body for immoral purposes, but she had to mingle and dance with whoever bought the nickel tickets. Jed had learned that she was originally from a little cowtown in Texas that died after a bad dust storm. Her folks had moved west, but Apaches had killed them both when they had camped with some Mexicans on the Pecos one afternoon. She had survived, moved on alone, winding up in Pima Flat where she'd had to sell her team and goods. Now she was working, trying to save enough to go to California where she had an aunt, cousins. Jenny Lee Carter, slightly older, had befriended Willa, seen to it that she got the job, stayed out of trouble with the roughnecks. Jenny Lee had approved when she had taken to Jed, so Willa had decided to give up her virginity two nights before. Now, she was glowing, happy, with hours to kill before she had to go to work as a dance hall girl.

"Might be just talk," said Jed, wrapping his arm around her waist. "Want to get something to eat down the street?"

"That's not what I want."

Jed grinned. Jenny and Willa had to live upstairs over the saloon, but he had a room in the hotel proper. And that's where he had deflowered her.

"Shall we, then?" Jed smiled, standing up. He took Willa's hand in his own.

"I'd like to get away from the hotel for a while. Could we go someplace else?"

The bartender stepped up to them. "Why don't you two ride on out to my place. You can have some privacy there."

"That'd be great," said Randall. "If you wouldn't mind."

Yire waved a bar towel in reply. He had worked the long bar for three years and had never seen so many strangers in town at once without a cattle drive or a horse trade going on. Pima Flat was a quiet trail town, serving ranchers, drifters, surveyors, land speculators, a way stop for the stage. It had known trouble, but only incidentally. Minor trouble. A fist-fight or two, a killing over a card game once. Nothing like what he felt was brewing now. He had seen the older Coker come in with his son that first night, and the other five hardcases. That's when he had first known that Pima Flat might be used for a showdown. He still didn't know why these seven men had come to town, but the name that cropped up most often was "Gunn." And even T.O. had mentioned it that morning.

Seven men after one man?

Yire walked to the end of the long bar after Jed and Willa left. He sat down. The place was empty now. The stuffed deer heads, the buffalo and elk heads stared into space and the small stage with its musty curtains seemed to breathe in the afternoon heat. Yire was a married man now and his wife wanted a kid. If there was trouble in Pima Flat he didn't want any part of it. Trouble had a way of spreading out, affecting even those who were the most pacific.

Gunn.

A name he'd never heard until a couple of days ago. Now it echoed in his brain. A bad omen, too. Gunn. Gun. Pistol. Rifle. A hell of a name. And seven men here to kill him.

Another claiming to be his friend. And Lassiter hiring him on to break horses. Gunn must be one hell of a man. He was sure in a heap of trouble.

Yire lifted his roly-poly frame from the pickle barrel seat and went over to the cash drawer in front of the mirror. On a shelf underneath was a sawed-off double-barreled Greener. Next to it, a .32 Smith & Wesson revolver. He checked the chambers in the S & W, then cracked the barrels on the shotgun. Both loaded. He slipped the revolver from its holster and stuck it in his belt, down below the top of the apron.

If there was going to be a shootout, it would probably be right here in the saloon.

Yire looked at the front door, wondering if that would be the way Gunn would come in. Then he glanced at the lobby entrance. That could be the way. Or, maybe Gunn would come in the back door and just start shooting.

Suddenly, Tom Yire was sick to his stomach.

He thought of his wife, Marina and of the extra room he was building on their adobe.

It was suffocating inside the saloon.

Suffocating, and hollow as a tomb, as he waited for a man named Gunn to show up and meet death head-on.

Gunn, whoever he was, didn't have a prayer in hell.

He was outnumbered and outgunned.

Gunn outgunned?

It seemed funny and Yire started to laugh.

And then he stopped laughing because there was nothing funny about any of it. He might have to take sides if trouble broke out and which side would he chose? Randall seemed like a halfwit sometimes, and he'd never met Gunn. But he was breaking horses for little or no pay if he was at the Lazy L. He sounded like a loser.

The Coker bunch, on the other hand, seemed to know just what they were doing. They weren't in a hurry, either. They just waited. Like vultures on the rimrock.

Waiting.

Waiting for a man named Gunn.

CHAPTER FIVE

Gunn tried to leave, but T.O. made him wait until supper. And then supper was put away and T.O. got sick. Real sick.

They were having coffee when Lassiter doubled up in his chair like a man kicked in the groin.

Esmerelda screamed.

Gunn knocked over his coffee cup as he reached out to keep his friend from falling face forward on the floor.

T.O. slumped over and went down, Gunn's grip on him too light to hold his weight.

"Pa!"

Gunn scraped his chair away from the table and managed to bend down to help Lassiter. The man's face was ashen as Gunn turned him over. There was blood on the corners of his mouth. His eyes were closed and there was a lump just above his temple where he had hit his head on the wood floor.

"I'm going to stretch him out, L.D. Fetch some brandy and smelling salts if you have them."

"I—I don't know . . ."

Gunn looked up at her. She sat frozen to her

chair, her face flushed crimson, her eyes wide. She was in shock, he saw.

He stretched T.O. out, listened to his heart. It was beating. Feebly. Fresh blood spilled from the old man's mouth. Gunn shielded this sight from his daughter.

"I'll get him to his bed. Can you turn down the sheets? Move, girl, move!"

As if lashed by a whip, L.D. sat up straight, gripped the table with a white hand and staggered from the room. Gunn heard a door creak, the rustle of sheets. He put his arms under the stricken man and lifted him gently. T.O. didn't weigh much, but it was dead weight. Gunn heard the man's breath rattling through blood. He would have to get something down his throat. Brandy, whiskey, water. Otherwise, T.O. might strangle on his own blood.

He carried the unconscious man into the bedroom. Esmerelda stood by the bed as if in a trance. The color had now gone from her face. She was breathing very fast. Gunn thought she might faint.

"Sit down!" he ordered.

He lay T.O. on the bed, loosened his belt.

"Watch him," he said, trying to make Esmerelda understand, snap her out of her hysteria. At least she wasn't screaming. Rather, she was in a waking stupor, stunned by what she had witnessed. Gunn left the room in long strides and went to the whiskey cabinet in the front room. He knew where T.O. kept his stock. He found some *aguardiente,* a shot glass. It would have to do.

When he returned to T.O.'s bedroom, Esmerelda was composed enough to have pushed a pillow under her father's head and slipped off his boots.

"What's wrong with him?" she asked, her voice quavering.

"Don't know yet."

"What's that blood on his mouth?"

"You ask too many questions. Help me prop him up. I've got to get this brandy down him. It might kill him, or it might do him some good."

"Who do you think you're talking to? You can't order me around like . . ."

Gunn slapped her. Hard.

Esmerelda staggered back, drew a hand to her cheek. She blinked her eyes in outraged shock.

Gunn glared at her.

"Either help me," he said, "or get the hell out of the room!"

He slid an arm under T.O., tried to prop him up. Esmerelda, forgetting her anger for the moment, bent down to help from the other side. They got T.O. up into a sitting position. Gunn pulled the cork out of the bottle with his teeth and pried the old man's mouth open with the glass neck. He dribbled a few drops of brandy onto T.O.'s tongue.

"If you hurt him, I'll kill you," hissed Esmerelda.

"Shut up," spat Gunn.

He poured more brandy into T.O.'s mouth. This time, Lassiter swallowed. His body shuddered. He choked. His eyes opened briefly. Gunn eased him back down on the pillow.

"He's breathing some better," said Gunn.

Esmerelda looked at her father, winced.

"I—I didn't know he was this sick. What he said out there. About the cancer. Is it bad?"

"About as bad as anything can be, I reckon. He's

probably been hiding a lot of pain for a long time. Maybe he was waiting for you to get back so he could just let go."

"Is—is there anything I can do?"

Gunn shook his head, stood up straight. There was just no easy way to break it to her. Lassiter was dying. He might not last the night. Or he could linger on, shriveling up inside as the cancer ate away at him. Either way, it was going to be tough for her.

"Make him comfortable. Get some Laudanum from a doc."

"Is he dying?"

Gunn turned away from her. His guts were quivering. That one brief look when Lassiter's eyes had opened told the story. There was a glaze of the old man's eyes. A film like the gloss of death.

"I don't know," he said, striding toward the door. "I'll be outside if you want to talk. Sleep's the best thing for him now."

Esmerelda watched the big man leave. Still in a state of shock, she realized with a sickening impact, that she was more alone now than in any other time in her life. She felt vulnerable, exposed. She worried at her lower lip, wondering at how her life had changed. All the time in Texas she had dreamed of coming back home, helping her pa take care of the ranch, ride horses, maybe raise cattle. Then, she would meet a nice young man, settle down and build a home next to the Lazy L. The dream was perfect. Except things never worked out the way you imagined them. Seeing the land again, after so long away from it, jarred her sense of reality. It wasn't the same. It was hotter, dryer, more inhospitable than she remembered. And now this. Her pa harboring a hidden growth and probably dying, almost before she had gotten to know him again.

She thought of Gunn. He was another unexpected part of the world she had come back to; a strange man who grew stranger by the minute. He had lied to Randy Coker about his name. If she hadn't heard her father and Gunn talking she would not have known his real name either. And Randy had said he was going to kill Gunn. For an injustice done to his father. Who was right? It was confusing. At first she had thought Gunn an interloper, a stranger interfering in her plans, her dreams. Now, seeing the way he had taken care of her father, she wasn't so sure. Yet, he had slapped her, been rude to her. What kind of a man was he? Did she deserve such treatment? Perhaps. She had lost her senses seeing her father in such pain, glimpsing his own mortality. Fear had driven her over the edge. Fear for her own future, fear of losing her father at this very important time in her life.

Quietly, Esmerelda began stroking her father's forehead. Tears welled up in her eyes. She let them come. Her hand strayed to his mouth, touched the bloody corners, felt his chin. He seemed so frail, just then. So helpless. What could she do for him? His face was the color of ashes, his breathing shallow, unsteady, threaded with a harsh grating sound.

She left the door to the bedroom open, went to the kitchen. She returned with water and a cloth. She cleaned up the drying blood on her father's face and listened to his breathing for a long while.

"Pa," she whispered. "I—I love you. Please don't die. Please!"

Outside, Gunn stood near the corral, watching the horses he had broken. He heard her footsteps, but did not turn around. Smoke curled from a cigarette dangling from his mouth. The smoke stung his eyes.

"I'm sorry I shouted at you," she said softly, coming up behind him.

"You had a right. He's your pa."

"No. I—I was in a state. I never saw him like that. I didn't know."

"Neither did I."

"He's not going to make it, is he? I mean, I'm scared. I won't know what to do if he dies."

"No. You never know what to do when that happens."

"You know."

"It's different. Every time. With every person."

"Was Randy's father involved in your wife's death? I asked Pa about it before supper. He said that you were wronged. I didn't believe him then. I didn't want to believe him."

"It doesn't matter. I wouldn't get too attached to Randy Coker if I was you."

Esmerelda stepped in front of Gunn, leaned against the corral rail. She looked up at him, into his blue-gray eyes.

"You're going to kill him, aren't you? That boy?"

"He's man enough to carry a gun."

"He's still a boy. Not much older'n me."

Gunn watched the horses munching on the grain he'd put out. Others drank at the trough he had filled from the pump.

"I took care of the chores," he told her. "In the morning, they'll need grain. There's hay in the back shed. Enough to carry you through to Spring."

"I can handle it."

"There's thirty, forty head up on the creek. You'll have to check on them in a day or so."

Esmerelda knew then that her father would never get out of his bed. Gunn knew and he was telling her in his quiet voice that she would have to carry on. Yet how could she manage a broken-down ranch all by herself? She couldn't. Gunn knew she couldn't. She'd have to sell out, if she could, and then what? Where would she go? Back to Texas? Somewhere else for a fresh start? It was all so overwhelming.

"Could this ranch pay?" she asked, startled by her own boldness.

"Might. People need horses. Good horses. You'd have to hire a hand. It's too much for one person."

"Pa did it."

"He tried. I think he wanted all these horses brought down and broke so you'd have a stake after he was gone, L.D. You got any money?"

"A little. Pa set up an account for me in Tucson. He had some cash money in another one, I think. We lived very frugally."

"Good idea. I could help you out. I owe your pa something."

"No you don't. I know what you took as pay. He told me. One horse."

Gunn looked at Esquire. The horse had good legs, a deep chest. He could cross a river or two.

"He gave me a lot more than that." Gunn stepped on his cigarette, ground it into the dust.

He started to walk toward the tack room, but Esmerelda put out a hand, touched his arm.

"I—I don't want you to leave tonight. I know why you're going, but please don't go now. I couldn't handle it. Being alone with pa like this."

Gunn stopped, looked at her. She had softened. The light spun gold furls in her hair, streaked her face. The sun would be down soon. It was a bad time to be alone with a dying man.

"I can't stay until he dies, L.. If I do, the trouble will come this way."

"Just stay until morning. Please."

"I'll sleep outside."

"No," she said quickly. "Inside."

"It wouldn't be proper, ma'am."

Her face flushed a roseate glow as her temper rose once again.

"Don't talk to me about proper, mister! You . . . you . . . you killer!"

"Hey, L.D. Back off! It's your reputation I'm thinking about."

"And who's going to know way out here? Pa? Do you know why he sent me away to Houston in the first place? No, of course not! What do you think I am, Mister Gunn? Some lily-white sister of mercy, raised in a convent? He had a hired hand here before. He tell you that?"

"No, but I don't see . . ."

"It's your turn to shut up! I'm not finished yet."

Gunn backed away, held up his hands, palms out, in mock surrender. He liked her spunk. Her eyes flashed when she was angry and her face was most becoming, rosy as a stone bluff in the morning when the sun first touches it with peach.

"Well, this hand was nineteen years old. An orphan

Pa found in Tucson, half Indian, half French. He was good with horses, but he was good with women too. At least I thought so. I bedded him one day, or tried to, and Pa caught us. He fired Pierre and shipped me off to Houston. But I'll tell you something, Mister Gunn. I wanted that boy real bad. And if Pa hadn't caught us I'd of probably run off with him. I saw what he had and he kissed me enough times on the mouth to make me know there was something better than that we could do. Understand?"

"That don't make you a hard woman, Esmerelda," Gunn said quietly. "You were just spoonin', that's all."

"That's all? I had my clothes off, my panties down and Pierre was naked as a jaybird. A minute more and I'd have been the woman I wanted to be."

"Jesus," Gunn said softly.

"What?"

"Nothing. I didn't say anything. You just surprised me, that's all. I thought you were a nice girl, raised proper. But you aren't bad, no matter what you say. Passion is passion and who's to say when a person has reached his moral limit? I guess your Pa was pretty mad, though."

"Hell, Gunn. He was mad only because Pierre was a half-breed. He didn't give a damn about me rolling in the hay. He just wanted better, that's all."

Gunn sucked in a breath, kicked at an imaginary clod in the dirt.

"I'll sleep on the floor in the front room," he said. "In the morning, I'll hay and grain the horses and be on my way. No ifs, ands or buts."

Esmerelda's anger subsided and she smiled. She

was pretty even then, he thought. There was no way she wasn't pretty, in fact. But she was some strange young lady. One of the strangest he'd known.

Gunn spread his bedroll on the floor in the front room. He shucked his boots, stripped out of his clothes, then crawled under the soogan. He put his boots under the bedroll, lapping them so that they formed a soft pillow for his head. He reached over to the small table where the oil lamp burned. Shadows flickered in the room; copper light glazed the window panes. T.O. was sleeping peacefully. He hadn't seen L.D. for the past hour, assumed she had gone to bed, exhausted from her trip, the events of the day. His fingers touched the brass disc to turn down the wick.

He hesitated, listening to the soft pad of footsteps. She came into the room, her nightgown rustling against the floor, bare legs.

"You don't have to sleep on the floor," she said. There was a low husk in her voice. Like a cat in heat. Her breasts pushed against the bodice of her gown, mounded above the cloth like ripening melons. The light danced on her skin, struck diamonds in her eyes.

"I'm used to hard ground," he said.

"Not tonight, Gunn. I want you to come to my bed."

He stared at her, his eyes narrowing. She looked like a child. Then, a woman. He saw the outlines of her thighs underneath the thin cloth of her gown. Saw her ankles, her naked feet.

"Your pa would skin me."

"No. Not you. He likes you. You're the man he would want me to have. The one he'd like to be the first."

Gunn swallowed. The lump in his throat refused to go down. He felt a tightening in his loins. A brief heat like a desert wind suddenly rising out of nowhere.

"It's a big step, L.D. I'll be gone in the morning."

"I don't care. You're here tonight. I want you."

Gunn's Adam's apple moved again. The lump slid a little, closed off his air. His scalp tingled. Esmerelda took a step toward him, smiled wanly. He saw the dark patch between her legs, the mysterious triangular brush nestled between her thighs. A surge of feeling shot through his groin, like an electric charge.

"A substitute for Pierre?"

"No. I've forgotten about him. A boy. You're a man. Gunn, don't talk about it. I'm full of nerve now. I want you bad. Real bad. It hurts."

Gunn propped himself up on one arm, ran a hand through his hair. He tried to look away, but he couldn't. She was beautiful. Her eyes bore into him. He saw the yearning in them.

He reached back to the lamp, turned the wick down. The flame sputtered out. Gunn rose from his bedroll, kicking the soogan aside. He went to her in the dark, found her. She wore perfume. He swallowed hard. The lump slid down his throat as he took her in his arms, kissed her.

"Yes," he husked. "I guess you do want me, L.D. It's right mutual."

CHAPTER SIX

Esmerelda's bed was small, soft.

There was room enough for just the two of them.

In the dark, she slid out of her gown. She reached and pulled the curtains aside. Soft silver light slanted into the room, bathed the bed in a hazy glow. He saw her body, then, all shadowy hollows and graceful angles. The nest between her legs, her pert young breasts rising from a smokey plane. He lay close beside her, his manhood rigid against her leg, seeping hot clear liquid onto her flesh.

He touched a nipple with the tip of his finger.

She spasmed as if he had burned her.

"Ooooh," she sighed.

He cupped her breast to assess its size and shape. It was perfectly made, pliant, yielding. Her loins squirmed. He bowed his head, took the nipple in his mouth. Tongued over it delicately.

"Oh, yes," she breathed.

She arched her back, thrusting her breasts upward. Gunn laved them both with tongue until she sank back down on the bed, spreading her legs.

"I want you," she said.

He touched her between the legs, sending an electric shock through her loins.

"Soon, L.D. Feasting should not be hurried."

"Yes, oh, yes."

He caressed her furred mound, plied the pliant lips with his finger. She squirmed, the need in her building, growing more urgent with each stroke of his hand. He kissed her tummy, the insides of her legs. She writhed beneath him, goosebumps rising on her flesh where he touched her.

"Gunn, you're torturing me," she gasped.

"Want me to stop?"

"No, for god's sake, don't stop. But what are you doing to me? I—I've never felt anything like this."

Gunn buried his face in her muff. His tongue slithered into the sex-crease, stabbed at the tiny shoot buried inside her. He pulled it between his lips, felt it trob and swell.

Esmerelda screamed as electricity jolted her. Her body bucked with a sudden spasm.

Gunn knew she was ready.

"That's what I was doing to you," he said.

Inside, she was like cream. He slid smoothly through her portal, clear to the barrier.

"Oh," she said. "Oh."

"You are a virgin, L.D."

"I told you I was."

"Still, a man doesn't always know for sure."

"Does it make any difference?"

"Not to me."

"Well, not to me, either. Not anymore. I can feel you there. Inside me. It—It's wonderful. You're wonderful."

"Shhh! Don't talk so much."

Gunn bore down, hammered softly at her maidenhead, softening it for the final assault, the last thrust that would rip it asunder. He felt it loosen, stretch. Esmerelda was unmindful of his technique. She was lost in a rapt world of her own. The bed sheets were roiled to a froth of blankets and sheets as she thrashed, bucked, writhed, squirmed. Her back arched and her legs flew up in the air as Gunn smacked his groin against hers, his hardness boring through steaming folds of flesh.

The end of her virginity was quick, virtually painless.

Gunn thrust quickly, and his cock shot through the hymen, rupturing it.

"Oh, yes, Gunn, yes!" she screamed softly. "I feel it! I feel it!"

She lost count of the orgasms ripping through her flesh. She didn't know the name for the sensation, but knew that she had experienced something unique and womanly. Something so special that even her aunt had never mentioned it to her. Now, she wanted to rush out into the world, and shout it to everyone. It was not dirty or shameful, but beautiful! It was not sinful, but the most wonderful feeling anyone could have! Her body felt clean, alive. She felt as if great weights had been lifted from her heart. Weightless, she floated in the rapture of those moments when Gunn was thrusting deep inside her, burrowing through to the deepest part of her, opening up hidden springs, triggering fresh electric charges that blossomed in her mind like marvelous and strange fireworks. Gunn had been right. There was no need to talk anymore. What was there to say that anyone but they would understand? Certainly she did not have a vocabularly for the sensations she was experiencing. There were no words to describe how she felt right now, a man inside her, over her, part of her, one with her. It seemed as if they were one person, not two. Yes, it was most strange, most wonderful. She looked up, saw his shadowy face, a face lit only by starlight and the faint glow of the moon. He seemed like a god to her then. He was performing miracles. Secret miracles that no one had ever so much as whispered about to her in all the years of her childhood. Yet her experience, she reasoned, must be common to all humans, all beings. Mating, coupling, soaring like a bird while lying on a bed.

Gunn stroked her slow, then fast. He imagined what she must be thinking. It was good. For her, for him, for both of them. She was eager, but not experienced. Yet now that her maidenhead was gone, she had all the experience she needed—feeling itself.

She would marry someday, settle down. But she would have this memory. Just as he had his memory of Laurie. It would stand her in good stead. If she married a clod, maybe she could teach him what to do, the places to touch, the rhythms that pleased her. As Laurie had done with him.

All women were different. They were the same, but different. Each had her own pet desires, special places that needed touching, caressing, fondling. That was what made them different, made them interesting. One might turn inside out when touched on the inner thigh. Another might melt when kissed behind the ear. With woman it was all touching, and a man who took the time to find out a woman's special preferences was the man who was also happy lying with a woman. Laurie had taught him that, too, even though she had never expected him to known any other woman.

Esmerelda had just made the transition from girl to woman. He had no doubt that she had been ready for a long time. He was somewhat grateful that he had been the key to unlock the door for her. But it could just as well have been Randy Coker. Or Jason Coker. Or anyone at all. L.D. was special, though. She was the daughter of a man he called friend. She had some cards stacked against her. No mother, for one: A dying father, for another. And, Randy Coker had sniffed her out. Good name for him: Randy. Horny. At stud. But he had seen good old boys like Randy before. They were like rabbits. They saw a woman, got her in the soogan and jumped her. No talk, no loving, just plain old fucking. A straight pipe to the well. In and out. Get the nuts off and hop onto the next one down the road. Well, men were not so different. But sometimes it paid to spend a little time with a woman. Especially the first time. You never knew what might happen later on. People had a way of cropping up again and again during a man's life. Especially women. Even the ones that got married sometimes got widowed, or divorced, or just ran off, looking for the man they knew when love was good and sex was good.

Gunn let Esmerelda have her head. He played her, but he turned her loose, too. She was like a young colt, frisky on new, unsteady legs. She jumped, bucked, ran, slowed. He matched her rhythms, brought her along on his own, at times. She thanked him by holding him tight, squeezing him, kissing him and giving him pleasure in her warm loins.

He stood it as long as he could.

His own passion strained on its leash like a ravenous tiger at mealtime.

"Kiss me hard," she breathed, as he rested his loins in hers. "You're not satisfied yet."

"Some."

"Not completely."

"No, L.D."

"I know that much," she said.

"You know a lot."

"What was she like?"

"Who?"

"Your woman. Your wife."

"You still talk too much, Esmerelda."

"I know. I just feel . . . well, that I may be pleasuring myself too much and that you aren't . . . happy."

"I'm happy. Just brace yourself."

She took a breath, squeezed his shoulders with fierce hands. He felt a surge of pleasure.

"A man can only . . . can only feel like I do once. When you do it. When we do it."

"Do what?" Gunn teased her, floating there, sunk in her womanhood, basking in her liquid heat.

She hesitated, her lips forming words that wouldn't be spoken, her mind trying to find the symbols that could translate to speech, to words.

"Love."

"Love?"

"Are you making fun of me?"

"No. Is that the only word you know?"

"The only decent one."

"Say the one that's not decent."

He waited for her to say it. He waited a long time while she searched his eyes with hers. He plumbed his cock inside her in a slow rhythmical series of thrusts, then stopped. Waited some more.

"I can't say it," she said.

"You can. Words can't hurt you. Words are not bad."

"This one is."

"Oh? Which word?"

"Gunn, you're playing with me."

"Yes," he husked, plumbing her again. Dipping deep into her boiling springs. Surging through her quivering flesh to the mouth of her womb. He held her there, skewered on the end of his manhood and felt her tremble all over. Then he pulled his cock back out as if to withdraw it completely.

"Fuck," she said, her voice so soft he could barely hear the word.

"Yes. A good word. An old word. A word with blood and meat in it."

"Good women don't say such words."

"Who told you that, L.D.?" He put his arms under her back, drew her close to him. He slid back inside, into the warm coils of her pulsing flesh. "It's not so. A real woman says what she wants to when she's making love. She speaks about what she feels and she uses the words that are the most simple. She makes her man feel what she feels. Or tries to. A man can never feel like that, I know. You asked about my wife. She said the words. She was a very pure woman. She was not wanton, nor mean. She knew how to give and get, and how to get back."

He felt her fingers press into her shoulder blades, strike the bone.

"Yes," she said urgently, "I know what you mean. Fuck me, Gunn. I want you to fuck me and fuck me."

He waited, holding steady inside her.

Until she sighed and began grinding her loins against his. Until her hips moved in a new gentle rhythm. Until her sex-cleft clasped him and her mound pushed up against him, burying his cock deep inside her. Until she began to love him from below in the way he had showed her with his own loin motions. Until she surrendered to him and conquered him.

Gun slipped out of bed in the pre-dawn dark. Esmerelda lay curled up in a ball like a baby possum. He kissed her gently on the cheeks and tiptoed out of the room with his boots in hand.

T.O. lay awake, staring at the ceiling when Gunn looked in on him. His eyes were invisible, hollowed out by the dark shadows in the room.

"Gunn?" the old man croaked.

"Yeah. How you doin', T.O.?"

"Am I alive?"

"You're talking."

"L.D.? Asleep?"

"Yeah." Gunn shifted his weight. His socks squished onto the floor.

"She take you to bed?"

"T.O., that's private business."

"Good. She could do worse. That kid. Coker."

"She's a good girl, T.O. I'm going into the Flat. Anything I can get you before I go?"

T.O. struggled to a sitting position. He looked frail and ghostly in the dim light.

"I've got a pain in my gut that burns like fire."

"Want some water?"

"No. Jesus. I'll just ride it on out. Will you be back?"

I'll be back."

"Good," said T.O., sinking back down. Gunn went over to him, felt his pillow. It was damp. He took the old man's hand, squeezed it.

"I'll feed and water the stock before I go."

"Luck, Gunn. Maybe I'll see you bye and bye."

"Maybe," Gunn husked. He left the room, the sour scent of nightsweat.

Esquire skipped along the road, frisky as a colt. The sun peached the stone hills, crept along the land lighting up the mesquite, the yucca, the saguaros.

Gunn held the horse in. There was no hurry, and he had not yet learned any gaits. But Esquire was a natural. A high-stepper this morning, full of ginger root and the tang of the air before the sun boiled it, turned it to hard grit and red dust.

Coker was there, in Pima Flat.

Not the son, but the old man. He didn't care about Randy. If he got the way, then the boy would have to take his chances. But it was Jason Coker he was after. To finalize something. He was like the cancer that ate up T.O.'s insides. Still breathing, still working on him from the inside. Where he couldn't see him. He had cut him out once, but now he was back, growing, ravenous.

So, there was no justice in the world after all.

The Mexicans knew that, and now he knew. Coker should have been castrated and gutted before a jury of his peers. Instead, he was sent to prison. A prison from which he had escaped. Yet Coker had started a chain of events that led to the murder of his wife, Laurie, the destruction of his ranch. Coker had killed something but the courts said he was not guilty of murder. Not of the murder that mattered.

So, if there was no justice in the world, why bother with Coker? Just ride on past and let him chase shadows.

No, there was justice. At times.

Gunn patted the Colt .45 on his hip. It was snug in its holster. Loaded in five of the six cylinder holes. The empty one contained a rolled up pair of bills, a ten and a twenty. The Winchester hung from its scabbard, slapping against the saddle. It was loaded, the firing chamber empty. A single cock and it would be lethal.

These were all he needed. These and his wits.

Pima Flat shimmered in the sun as he crested the hill.

Down there, the Cokers were waiting. The pup and the old boar. And others too, he reckoned.

But Jed Randall was there too. An ally.

As he let Esquire have his head once again, Gunn felt a prickly scratching in his gut. A warning.

Pima Flat was another destiny in his lone path.

Death was waiting there.

But whose?

CHAPTER SEVEN

Pima Flat lay sprawled in the sun, a collection of adobes, half-mud, half-wood houses, saloons, the San Carlos Hotel and Elk's Head Tavern connected to it, El Pozo Seco, where the hardcases hung out, a stage stop, a few other businesses that seemed to be bracing themselves for the onslaught of afternoon heat.

Gunn rode in openly, headed for the Elk's Head, which was part of the hotel, but a separate business. Across the street, El Pozo Seco buzzed with talk and the clink of glasses. He tied up his horse at the hitching rail and walked into the cool log and adobe room. It was quiet, with only one silver-haired man at the bar. The bartender was busy polishing the bottles on the back bar.

Gunn took up a position where he could see the front door on the street, the door to the lobby, the stairs going up to the balcony and the way out back. Tom Yire noted the careful positioning, ambled over to serve him.

"You wouldn't be Mister Gunn, would you?" he asked quietly, his voice just above a whisper.

"I might be. Who's askin'?"

"I'm a friend of Randall's. Tom Yire's the name."

"Jed here?"

"Not at the moment. If you be the man he's lookin' for I'll send you out there."

"I'm Gunn."

Yire grinned, stretched out a hand. Gunn took it. The two shook hands.

"A beer if it's cool," Gunn said, "and have one for yourself."

"Cool enough and thank you."

The man at the other end of the bar finished up his drink, went into the hotel. Gunn and Yire were alone.

"You know about Coker and his bunch," said Yire, bringing two big glasses foaming with amber beer. The beer was cool enough, smelled of a dank cellar and pottery as Gunn lifted it to his lips. He drank, remembering that he'd had no breakfast. Suddenly, he was starved as the beer went down into his stomach.

"I know. That's why I'm here. Jason Coker in the hotel?"

Yire nodded, leaned over the bar conspiratorially. Briefly, he told Gunn about Coker and his bunch coming into town, asking questions about him. Then, he told him about Randy speaking to Randall.

"Randall figured to give you a chance to catch your breath and I told him to stay at my place. You got a bad bunch here, more'n you two can handle at once."

Gunn thought about that. Seven men, all tolled

and tallied. Young hardcases, tough, mindless, for the most part, with Randy at the lead. And back of them, Jason himself, calling the shots. Pulling the strings.

"Any of Coker's men up and about?"

Tom pointed across the street, towards El Pozo Seco, the dry hole, in English.

"Two of 'em are over there, jawin'," he said. "Martin and Langley."

"They'll keep." Gunn was about to ask where the bartender lived so he could look up Jed Randall when two women came in from the hotel entrance. They were pretty, whispering and giggling like schoolgirls. One of them made him look twice. She was dark-haired, blue eyed, petite of bone, but tall. She smiled at him and he felt a twinge in the region of his heart. The other was blonde, buxom, fair haired, with apple-red rouge on her cheeks. She, too, had blue eyes, but they were pale, like his own and vacant as a doll's.

"Buy us a drink?" said the blonde one, bold as fire.

"Sure. Tom?"

Tom frowned, but poured white wine for the ladies. They flanked Gunn, and the blonde one began playing with his arm.

"I'm Gretchen" she said. "Gretchen Lovelace."

Gunn nodded, turned to the dark-haired woman. "And you?"

"My name's Jenny Lee Carter and I think you're the craziest man I ever saw." She had a soft drawl and, up close, he saw that her mouth dimpled when she talked. She had an appealing, heart-shaped face.

Ringlets of curls hung in front of her ears. She smelled faintly of perfume. Unlike Gretchen, who reeked of it. But both girls were clean and friendly. It wasn't a bad start.

"Yeah, I've been called crazy, but not so quick on first acquaintance."

Gretchen squeezed Gunn's arm, demanding he turn his attention toward her. He stared into her pale eyes, scanned her plum cheeks.

"Old Nappy was in here, the gray-haired gent. Says you was the one what come to face all those young bucks who rode in here a few days ago. Nappy's taking bets that you'll be in a pine box by sundown."

"Did you bet with him?" Gunn asked.

Gretchen giggled, dipped her eyelashes.

"No, silly. But we wanted to see what you looked like. Why you're too handsome to die so young. Why don't you come upstairs with me and at least have a good time before those boys shoot you full of holes."

"Gretchen!" hissed Jenny Lee. "That's awful talk! Be nice!"

Gunn didn't mind. Gretchen was friendly and she seemed to be bubbling over with life. In a hard rock town like Pima Flat that was unusual enough. Jenny Lee seemed more reserved, but no less fun-loving. She had beauty that was rare and he wondered why she was living so far off the beaten track. He wanted to talk to her, quietly, privately, but Gretchen drew all of his attention toward her. She was, he accepted, clinging. Very clinging.

Gretchen told Gunn what they did for a living.

Dance-hall gals. She made sure he didn't confuse them with soiled doves, fallen women, but he wasn't so sure the distinction was that clear. Gretchen seemed eager to take him to her room and let him wallow on her body, but he had other things on his mind. While he wasn't pushing for a showdown so soon, he didn't want to be distracted from his mission. His first order of business was to find Jed and see what he was facing. Jed might help, or he might want to ride clear of this trouble. It was private trouble anyway. Gunn wouldn't ask him to help. He'd just see what Jed had to say, and if he wanted to ride on back to Tucson, that was fine. He couldn't ask the man to mix into his own personal troubles.

Tom came over, leaned close to Gunn.

"Those two boys are coming over," he said. "Don't turn around."

Gunn stiffened. Jenny Lee looked at Tom with wide eyes, but did not turn around.

Gretchen, who had heard Yire, stold a glance toward the front door. Quickly, she put her arm in Gunn's as if they were old friends. Then, to his surprise, she reached up and pulled his hat brim down, shielding his face.

Slicker Langley and Jack Martin were already three sheets to the wind. They walked to a table along an invisible crooked line, bumping into each other, stumbling over a chair leg. They sat down heavily.

"Let's have some fuggin' service in here," shouted Martin. Then he saw Gretchen and grinned idiotically. "Oh, sorry, lady, I got to watch my fuggin' tongue."

Martin started laughing, then, and Langley glared at Gretchen.

"Who you got with you, Miss Lovelace?" Langley slurred. "New beau?"

"Why it's my cousin in from Santa Cruz," she lied. "I haven't seen him in nigh a year."

Tom stood near Gunn.

"Maybe you better give me directions to your place," Gunn said, his voice pitched low. "Those boys are apt to start something without any good reason."

"I—I know the way," said Jenny quickly. "Please. Let me take you there. He's with my friend, Willa, anyway."

"Be okay, Tom?"

Yire nodded darkly.

"Gretchen, you stay here, keep those men occupied while we leave," said Jenny.

Gretchen nodded, sipped her wine. Reluctantly, she released her grip on Gunn's arm.

Gunn and Jenny walked out the front door. For an instant, he looked at Martin full face. Their looks locked and froze. Langley swung around to see what Martin was looking at, but Gunn reached the door and opened it for Jenny. The batwing swung behind them.

Outside, Gunn asked Jenny if she wanted a buggy or a horse.

"I'll ride with you," she said. "Willa's got a surrey out at Tom's and I can ride back with her."

"Fine," said Gunn, lifting her onto the horse. She sat back of the pommel, her dress bunched up in her lap. She weighed less than a hundred pounds, he thought, and her ankles were as trim as a racehorse's.

He untied the reins, swung up in the saddle. Jenny put her arms around his waist. He felt her breasts against his back.

He touched his rowelless spurs to Esquire's flanks.

The horse loped easily down the street, away from the Elk's Horn.

A minute later, Langley staggered outside the saloon, shading his eyes as he peered after Gunn and Jenny.

"Hey you!" he shouted. "Hey you! Come back!"

Gunn didn't even turn his head.

"Shit," said Langley, and lurched back through the batwing doors.

He meandered to the bar, leered at Gretchen.

"If that was your kin, what's he doin' ridin' off with Jenny?"

Gretchen's face blanched as if dusted with flour. She drew back, in fear. Tom Yire came over to help if Langley got rough.

"Why, why she just wanted to go ridin', that's all."

"Who in hell was that Jasper?" Langley demanded, his tongue thick with the effects of strong drink.

"He didn't leave his name," said Yire.

"I thought he was your cousin or brother, Gretchen . . ."

"I was just foolin', Mister Langley. I never saw him before in my life."

Langley's eyes narrowed to feral slits. He glared at Gretchen, then at Tom.

"You're both lyin'," he drawled. "Lyin' in your godamned teeth."

He grabbed Gretchen's arm, twisted it.

"Don't she begged. "You're hurting me."

"I want his godamned name." Langley dug his fingers into her arm, twisting it even more radically until Gretchen winced in severe pain.

"Gunn," she gasped. "His name was Gunn."

"You bitch!" Langley drew back his left fist as if to plow it into her face. Yire leaned across the bar, put his hand up in front of Gretchen as if to shield her.

"You don't hit a woman, Langley. Not here. Now get out."

"Why you sumbitch . . ."

Yire stepped back, reached down and hauled up a sawed-off Greener. He cocked it. Both barrels.

"Back off, Langley."

Martin rose up from his chair, stood there, weaving in place.

". . . the hell's goin' on . . ."

Langley realized that he had made a mistake. He shook his head as if the act would sober him up instantly.

He released his grip on Gretchen's arm. His fingers left streak marks in her flesh. He scowled at Yire, then staggered toward Martin.

"Come on," he snarled. "We got to see Coker. That bastard Gunn's in town."

"Yeah? I don't see him."

"Godammit, Jack, sober up. Coker's goin' to be mad as a stepped on sidewinder. We're in shit up to our armpits."

The two men left, trying to walk on steady boots as they careened through the lobby entrance to the saloon. Yire watched them go, heard their boots boom on their stairs. He let the hammers down gently, put the shotgun down.

"Shouldn't we warn Gunn?" Gretchen asked.

Tom shrugged.

"He knows what he's facing, I guess. If not, Randall will tell him. Meantime, you'd better be scarce. No telling what those men will do when they find out you talked to Gunn."

"Huh? They wouldn't hurt a lady?"

Tom looked at her with pity.

"No. They might kill you though. Just out of danged frustration."

Jason Coker looked at Langley with a frosty stare. He listened to what he had to say and kept silent. Randy's face began to show his own rage. His skin flushed a glazed pink from collar bone to ear lobes as he heard Langley recount the events in the saloon.

"You had him! You had the bastard!" Randy screamed. "And you let him get away!"

"Hold on, Randy," said Jason quietly. "This is no time to lose your head."

Langley started to square off, drunk enough to draw on Randy Coker, but mindful that he wasn't out of the woods yet. Jack Martin sprawled on the couch in the hotel room, trying to keep everyone in focus. His head throbbed like a melon rolling down a rocky slope.

"Dammit, Pa . . ."

"I said shut up, Randy!"

Randy sulked.

Jason stood up with the help of his cane, walked to the window. He felt shut in, a prisoner. The window afforded him a chance to look outside, at least, see a world he could no longer enjoy. The years in prison had helped make him a recluse, but the game leg allowed him little freedom outside the big walls. He felt a strange excitement now. His prey was close. Gunn was within his grasp. Well, almost. He licked his lips. Anticipating the revenge that was to come. At last. It didn't matter that Langly and Martin had let him slip through. Gunn was here. Where he had gone was another matter, though. The man was like a fox. He had proved that in Colorado. On Black Mesa. Good men had gone down under his guns and that was still a mystery to some. But each man had his own time and Gunn's was about to run out. He wouldn't tuck his tail and light a shuck. Not Gunn. He came to fight, that was sure. Maybe it was just as well that Langley had been drunk. He might live to get in on the kill. Had he gone for Gunn in his condition, he would be dead now. Martin, too. Coker had no doubt of that.

Jason turned from the window, limped to the table where Randy sat. Langley stood near the door, leaning against the wall.

"You boys sleep it off," he said. "Come back here in four hours. Sober. Randy, you see that they keep their noses clean."

"But, Pa . . . I should go after Gunn. He's probably clean out of the country by now."

"No, son. He won't leave. He doesn't run from a fight. He left with a local woman, didn't he? Probably to find Randall. That's the one you should have watched. Instead, you let him slip through your fingers."

"Pa, he didn't go to his room last night."

"No. Then where did he go? That's what you should know. Because that's where Gunn is headed."

Randy saw the logic of it. He bit his tongue. He was angry, frustrated, confused. His father seemed to know so much, even without leaving the hotel room. And he, who was supposed to be helping his father, was not even sure of what to do next. His first thought had been to chase after Gunn, shoot him and come proudly back with the news of his victory. But Gunn had slipped out of the net and was casual as hell about it. Yet he had to know that they were there. He felt a fool, the way Gunn had gulled him out at the Lazy L. with that alias. He had fallen for it.

"I can find him, Pa," said Randy. "Just give me the chance. Randall and Gunn both."

"No. He's got that Carter woman with him. A good sign." Jason pulled a cigar from his pocket, bit off the end. "He's doing what we want him to do. His mind is on the woman. That's what we want. Let him play with the pretties, and we'll catch him off guard." Jason lit the cigar, blew a stream of blue smoke through his lips.

"But what if he doesn't come back? Maybe Randall's waiting for him outside of town. Maybe they're on their way to Tucson now. Laughing at us."

"No, Randy," said Jason. "He'll show up. Now

get these men out of here and put 'em to bed."

"We don't need no nursemaid," said Langley, lurching to his feet, kicking off from the wall. He tottered, about to fall forward. Jack Martin laughed low in his throat, rose from the couch.

"We damn sure need some shut-eye," he said. "Hell, Coker, we'll be fit in a couple hours."

Jason fixed Martin with a glare.

"The only reason you're alive now is because you let Gunn get away, Martin. You'll stand little chance against him sober, much less drunk."

"He didn't look like much," said Martin.

Jason turned away from him, his eyes frosty.

"Let's hope you say the same thing when you're looking down the barrel of his gun from the wrong side, Martin. If you get the chance. Gunn's fast. No matter what he looks like to you, he's fast on the draw."

CHAPTER EIGHT

Yire's adobe was almost invisible to the naked eye.

Tucked back in the rocks, it seemed part of the landscape. Huge piled-up boulders on either side, it drew shade to its walls for most of the day. Logs jutted out of the earthen walls. Flowers grew in pots on the patio and in the earth where the sun struck most frequently.

There was a hitchrail out front and when Gunn and Jenney Lee passed between the rocks, he saw that the narrow defile opened up behind the house. There was a corral and adobe stable. Jed's horse was visible, munching on a biscuit of hay. A sulky stood in the shade to one side of the house, leaning on its side-braces.

Laughter, male and female, came from inside the adobe.

"Hello the house," called Gunn.

Randall's face appeared in the doorway. He was shirtless, his hair tousled.

"Damn! If it ain't old Gunn? How'd you find me?"

"The lady here." Gunn thumbed toward Jenny

who was shielded by his bulk.

"Well, yeah, Jenny Lee. Welcome, welcome. Step down, Gunn, and have a glass of *tepache.*"

The adobe was cool.

Willa Gleeson curtsied when she met Gunn. She appeared to have dressed hastily. Her light brown hair fell over her shoulders, was tousled as Jed's. She wore a yellow dress and her blue eyes danced when she talked. Gunn thought she was very feminine, pretty, with a heart-shaped face much like Jenny's. But Jenny was darker, more alluring somehow.

Gunn tasted the *tepache,* prounounced it adequate, cool enough, but on the sweet side. The girls left the living room, to talk in the back bedroom while Gunn and Tom brought each other up to date. Their voices were pitched low so that the girls wouldn't hear. Needless, since they could hear the women chattering away at the other end of the adobe.

"I didn't know how serious it was," said Randall. "You and this Coker go back a ways."

"You see him?"

"No. Just his kid. Smart-ass."

"The young ones are dangerous too. Unpredicatable."

"Yeah. What you figger on doing? We could just ride on out of here, lose him and his bunch 'tween here and California."

"I could do that. Ever had a man chasing you, Jed?"

"Only when I was riding with you."

"You have to sit facing every door. You jump at every sound. You see a man with his hat brim pulled down, you're sure he's spying on you. You keep looking back over your shoulder until you get a crick in your neck. You sleep like a sack of potatoes in a spring wagon, up and down, up and down all night. You start picking fights with strangers. You hate everybody you see, just on general principals. You keep running and keep looking at your backtrail until finally you stop and beg someone to come up and start shooting. You don't care if you die, you just want to get it all over with."

"That happen to you?"

"No. To the men I've hunted. But I know what they went through. It's hell and I'll have no part of it. Coker's here. He wants to kill me. So, I figger Pima Flat's the place to get it over with."

"I don't like the odds, Gunn. Coker's got more'n a half dozen hardcases backin' him. Ever' damn one of 'em looks as if he'd shoot his own mother if she looked at him cross-eyed."

"Right now, we're outnumbered. I reckon I'll have to reshuffle the deck."

Jed leaned across the table, interested in Gunn's plan.

"I hate to ask you to do this, friend. You could get shot."

"I could die in bed, too. Or I could get kicked by a horse. Or snake bit. What's a friend for?"

"You sure, Jed?"

Jed grinned.

"I'm sure."

Gunn's eyes brightened.

"Did Jason Coker see you, know what you look like?"

"No, just the kid, and two other jaspers."

"Well, it might work. Might not."

"What's that, Gunn?"

"Far as I know, Coker just wants me. He probably knows you're a friend, since you asked about me, but it's me he wants to rub out. You're checked into the San Carlos Hotel?"

"Yep."

"Well, reserve a room for me. Make it loud and plain. Tell the clerk I'll be there in an hour. Tell the clerk I don't want to sign in, but will just go on up to the room. Get the key and go on up. To my room. Leave it unlocked and your pistol cocked. I'll whistle when I come up. No whistle, you shoot. Got it?"

"All right. I don't see what good this'll do, though. They'll just wait at the desk until you ask for your room number."

"I'll know the room number."

"Huh?"

"Tell the clerk I want Jason Coker's room, that he won't be needing it."

"I can't do that, Gunn. Hell, he'll laugh right in my face."

Gunn's jaw tightened. His gray eyes grew cloudy, dark.

"You make sure he doesn't laugh. Just get the key to Jason Coker's room. Know which one it is?"

"Yeah, six, I think. Opposite end of the hall. Hell, Gunn, he stays in there all the time. I see men going in and out, but never Coker himself. He has all his food and whiskey sent up to him."

"Well, before you go to the desk, he'll come down. See if there's any paper here and a pen or pencil. I'm going to see to it that Coker gets a message to get out of that room."

Randall got up, went to a desk, found a sheaf of papers, a pencil stub. Gunn wrote a hasty message, folded it.

"Now what?" asked Jed.

"Get Willa to leave it at the desk, or hire a messenger to deliver it personal to Jason Coker." Gunn wrote *JASON COKER* across the outside of the folded note. He gave it to Randall.

"What's it say?" asked Randall.

"It tells Coker I'm waiting for him at El Pozo Seco."

Randall scratched his head.

"Man, you got something up your sleeve, I'll say. I still don't see what good it'll do to be up in Coker's room. Like you say, I could get killed."

"I want him out in the open. Flushed like a quail. After you get the room key, you get all the furniture turned over, make it into a barricade, stay behind it until your hear me whistle. We'll just sit there and wait, see who shows up. If Coker comes back to his room, he'll have to expose himself. I'll get him. If he's dead, the rest will scatter."

"What about his kid?"

"I figure he'll be busy burying his pa."

Jed Randall and Willa Gleeson split up two miles from town.

Jed didn't want her to have any part of Gunn's plan. It was too dangerous. Instead, he told her to go back to the Elk's Head and he'd see her there that night. Pouting, she rode on ahead.

Jed began to sweat the minute he hit town. He rode the back streets, came up behind the barber shop.

He went in the back way.

Four or five men were there, waiting for haircuts. Another sat in the chair, his face lathered.

"We got a front door," said the barber.

'Sorry," said Jed. "Just wanted to know if anyone here wanted to make a dollar."

"Doin' what?" asked a grizzled old-timer on the bench.

"Delivering a message to the hotel."

"Whyn't you take it yourself?" asked the man, a prospector with a thick beard, dust caked on his unbathed skin.

"It's a surprise. All you have to do is give a piece of paper to the desk clerk and tell him it's important he deliver it pronto."

The old prospector cocked his head, scratched his beard. Jed dug out a dollar, dangled it in front of him.

"Casey, save my place," the old man said to the barber. "Be right back."

Jed gave the note to the old-timer, who promptly snatched the dollar out of Jed's hand. He didn't look at the note and Jed guessed that he probably couldn't read.

"You want a haircut?" Casey asked Randall.

"Maybe tomorrow." Jed left by the back way, conscious that the men had stared at him with their mouths open. His heart pounded in his chest and sweat made his palms slipper.

It wasn't over yet.

He rode to the livery stable, put his horse up, paid in advance. The afternoon was sleepy, hot, ridden with magpies and roadrunners, scented with flowers, reeking with sweat, the faint scent of malt, whiskey fumes as he took up a stand in the passageway between two buildings. There, he could watch the front of the hotel and see who entered, who left. And, too, he had a view of the cantina, El Pozo Seco.

It was a bad place to be.

People stared at him, made him nervous.

Jed wondered what Gunn would do in such a situation. Hide? Try to be inconspicuous? No, not in such a place. The town was slowed at this hour, but people were about. Standing there between two buildings just drew attention to himself.

Randall pulled his hat brim down, walked up on a board porch, sat down, leaned against the store front. He fished out a Barlow pocket knife, found a stray piece of wood, began whittling.

He glanced toward the Pozo Seco, then at the hotel.

Thought of Willa, who had been angry at having to ride into town alone. He could make it up to her later. Gunn was a rare man. He felt loyalty toward him, but couldn't define his reasons. It didn't matter. Gunn was straight. Such men were not common, especially in the West. Still, Jed didn't understand him, his life. The few times he had worked with him, he had almost regretted knowing the man. Gunn must have been born under a bad star. Or else, he was just particular unlucky. Particular unlucky.

Gunn mixed in when practical men would just tuck in the spurs and hideyho on down the trail. The man seemed to thrive on danger. He killed, but wasn't a killer. He fought hard and fair, but wasn't a fighting man. He loved the ladies, but didn't fall head over heels for them. And the women didn't hate him for lovin' and leavin'. Rather, he had a special quality about him that made them love him all the more.

Gunn was a man to ride the river with, hell or high water. He came out all right. He didn't look for trouble, but trouble found him. And when it did, he didn't back off. He met it head-on and kept on riding where he wanted to go.

Randall admired few men, but he admired Gunn.

Now, though, he wondered if Gunn might not have gotten into something too deep for him, even. Hardcases out to shoot him down, plant him in Boot Hill. A crazy kid and a jailbird pa.

Jed slivered off wood from a stick with his knife and glanced toward the hotel. He saw the old-timer come out, walk back toward Casey's Barber Shop on the opposite side of the street.

Flies buzzed. The afternoon hummed with flying insects. The sun beat down, and the air seemed to hold still as if waiting for something to happen. Down the street some one lazily plucked a guitar, tuned it up. Then it was quiet again.

Siesta time in Pima Flat.

A buzzard circled in the blue sky, so high Jed could barely see him. He heard a quail call far off and then, even it, became still. A man came out of the barbershop, feeling his face tenderly. He scratched the back of his neck, squinted into the sun and then walked toward El Pozo Seco where it would be cool and the beer wet.

Fifteen minutes went by.

Twenty.

Jed had whittled the stick to a sliver. He tossed it aside, wondering if the old coot had delivered the message to the desk clerk, if the clerk had delivered it to room six. Most of all, he wondered if Coker had fallen for it. This was not Jed's idea of a good time. Waiting. It would be nicer if he could be with Gretchen or Willa, lying on a soft bed with his boots off. A woman running her fingers over his skin, rubbing his forehead.

Jed began to doze.

Movement caught his eye.

The San Carlos Hotel! The front door swung open. A man came out, his hand hovering next to his pistol.

Bat Hudson!

Hudson looked up and down the street, turned and nodded to someone still inside the hotel. Then he glanced across to the El Pozo Seco. Jed thought he was going to cross the street and go inside. But instead, Bat walked toward the alley on the same side. There, he took up a position where his body was partly concealed. He did not draw his side arm, but waited.

Paul Burns came out of the hotel, glanced down at Hudson who nodded to him. Burns walked in the opposite direction, then stopped, stood behind two large pickle barrels in front of the mercantile store. He kept his eyes on the cantina.

Jed stared at the hotel entrance, licking his lips.

Pete Cantwell, whom he did not know, but had

seen from a distance, emerged from the hotel a few seconds later. He went across the street, stood next to the doorway of the El Pozo Seco.

His hand gripped his pistol butt, ready to draw it at an instant's notice.

Randy and Jason Coker stepped out on the boardwalk in front of the hotel. Jed could not hear them, but Randy leaned over and whispered something to his father. Jason nodded, pushed him out in front of him. Randy walked two paces ahead of Jason as the two crossed the street toward the cantina.

Just before they reached the middle of the street, Cantwell went inside the cantina, his pistol in his hand.

Jed smiled.

Jason Coker was taking no chances, but he was up a blind trail. Just as Gunn had wanted him to be. Whatever was in that note, it had brought Coker out into the open. Now, it was up to him to carry out the rest of Gunn's plan.

Cantwell reappeared in the doorway of the cantina.

"Not here yet, Coker!" he said loud enough for his voice to carry to Jed's ears. "It's okay to come in."

The Cokers went inside the saloon. Hudson and Burns converged from their stations and followed the others inside El Pozo Seco.

Jed rose, threw away the piece of wood he had whittled to a sliver. He pocketed his knife, walked briskly toward the hotel.

Inside, he strode to the desk, rapped loudly on the counter.

The clerk looked up from the dog-eared and worn copy of *Harper's* he was reading.

"Yes, Mister Randall? You lose your key?"

"No. I want a room for a friend of mine."

The clerk got slowly to his feet. He was a thin, balding man, stooped over so that he appeared even shorter than his five foot three inches of height. Hatless, the bald part of his pate glistened with beads of oily sweat. His lips were rimmed with brown tobacco stains. His skin was yellow with jaundice and he limped, favoring his kidney.

The clerk opened the ledger, shoved it toward the quill pen in its well.

"He'll have to sign or you sign for him."

"You can put down his name."

"Eh? What name is that?"

"Just put down the name Gunn . . ."

That was as far as Jed got.

He heard a rustling sound, turned to see a man sitting in a chair. A newspaper fluttered to the floor.

Jed whirled, his right hand darting toward the butt of his holstered pistol. Even as he reached for his Colt he knew it was too late.

Slicker Langley grinned, thumbed back the hammer of the pistol rising from his lap.

The big Remington .44 boomed. White smoke belched from the barrel.

Jed staggered. Pain shot through his shoulder. His gun hand went numb.

CHAPTER NINE

Jenny Lee looked at Gunn out of the corner of her eye, trying to appear as if she wasn't watching him at all.

But then, it happened again.

That feeling she got every time she looked at him. A lurch in her senses. Her brain filling with a whirlwind.

The tug in her stomach. The drenching cold that flooded her veins just before they heated up as if fire was pumping from her heart.

Her knees going weak, melting into jelly. Giving way, so that she thought she might tumble forward, sprawl awkwardly on the floor of Yire's adobe.

There was something about the man. She looked at his muscles in fascination. Rapt, as if struck dumb by a thunderbolt. When he moved, she felt herself moving with him, flowing beside him as if she belonged there, as if she had always belonged there.

Then, too, there was the matter of her heart. It beat wildly every time she looked into his pale eyes, or at his slightly cleft chin, saw the dimples at the corners of his mouth. Her heart seemed to stop at times. She was not sure of that. It may have been her breath, caught in suspension between her lungs and mouth. At times it felt as if her throat was filled with autumn leaves, or the fine desert silt blown up and into the air with the dust devils that traversed the land in late spring, early summer.

Jenny Lee Carter was twenty-three years old, frightened.

Frightened of growing old, of winding up as a spinster. Scared of being used up, tossed aside, left to wither in a town like Pima Flat. The fear was real. Haunting. Like the memories of her past life.

Born in 1855 in Illinois, she had never had solid roots. Her father, Earl Carter, had been restless, eager to push west with so many others who dreamed and read the flyers about cheap land, better opportunities somewhere beyond the Mississippi. Earl and his wife, Mattie, had left Illinois just before the War between the States had broken out, landing in Texas where their money had run out. Dreaming of Oregon and the sea, Earl had been diverted by the necessity of earning a living and found himself far south of the trails across the vast prairie when war was declared. A Northerner by disposition and choice, he had left his family in Wichita Falls, while he returned to Illinois to join up with the Union Army.

Earl Carter was killed in Jackson, Mississippi, just after he sent his wife some money he had inherited from an uncle. Mattie, with the money in hand and a letter from her husband's commanding officer telling of Earl's death by grapeshot, packed up her belongings and headed west, hoping to take up a new life in California. Instead, she was robbed of her money and murdered in El Paso. As she lay dying, she told Jenny Lee to go on with what was left of their money and find a place to live and grow. Jenny had less than $50 sewed into one of her dresses and she got as far as Pima Flat. That was a month ago. She had taken the job at the Elk's Head out of desperation, hoping to save enough money to take the Overland from Tucson to San Bernardino where she had an aunt.

Now, watching Gunn cleaning his rifle and pistol at the table, she realized that she had been swept up by circumstances for too long. She had moved too fast for grief to strike her. Now, the emptiness of her existence rose up to smother her. Being here, alone with a man, in a house that breathed her own longings, she was overcome with sadness and yearning. Gunn's hat was off, and his thick hair fell over his forehead, clotted at his neck. His corded muscles rippled under his skin as his arms moved, his hands lovingly smoothed the barrel of his Colt .45.

Gunn looked up, saw Jenny turn quickly away. He smiled.

"I'm sorry," he said. "Got lost in what I was doing. Didn't mean to be antisocial."

Jenny was too embarrassed to say anything.

"I mean," he said, "if you want to talk, I'm almost finished." He reloaded the Colt with five bullets, returned the weapon to its holster.

Jenny glided across the room, sat at the table. Her heart fought against the cage of her breast like a fluttering bird.

"I—I didn't want to bother you while you were busy," she said.

"It's all right. I'm not used to much company, I guess."

She looked at the gleaming Winchester on the table, smelled the oil. The stock had a high sheen to it.

"Are you really going to go up against all those men?"

"Don't see any way out of it."

"You could get killed."

"I reckon."

"Aren't you afraid?"

"Of getting killed?"

"Yes."

"I reckon there's better things, and worse. A man could get hurt, maimed, and end up being dependent on the world for a living. If you die, well, that's part of life, too."

"I would be afraid . . ."

Gunn leaned back in his chair, grinned wide.

Jenny's face was so serious, her gaze so intent, he could not help but smile.

"Well, I wouldn't want to go no earlier than was intended," he said, "but I reckon there's not much to worry about. If a man dies and doesn't go anywhere else after that, doesn't become a spirit as the Indians think, or an angel like the Christians believe, then he doesn't have any worry there, either. He's just dead and that's that. He goes back to the earth, to dust, to the worms."

Jenny shuddered.

"How terrible!"

"Jenny Lee, you worry too much. The Sioux now, they're a right smart bunch of peoples. When they kill an animal for food, why they're real polite and they thank the animal. They say, to the antelope, or the deer, or the buffalo: 'thank you brother, for giving up your life so that I can eat. Someday I will feed your brothers. So, they know what happens to a body after the spirit has left it. And they don't mind dying at all much after the age of twelve. By that time, they figure a man is grown enough to be grateful for life and give it up when the times comes. All the days after that age are considered gifts, more fullness to a life that's already plumb full."

"You—you make it sound almost beautiful. I didn't know the savages ever thought about such things."

"Well, they wouldn't much like to be called savages, especially by a people so savage they're trying to wipe them out, cheat them, starve them, shoot them like dogs and run them off their lands."

Jenny Lee looked at Gunn with new admiration. His voice was pitched low and she hung on his words like a child listening to a favorite story. No one had ever talked that way to her before. No one had taken her childish curiosity seriously until now.

"What will you do if you win?" she asked. "Where will you go?"

"West. To California. Or wherever my horse takes me."

"That's where I was going. To California. San Diego. But now I wonder if I'll ever get there."

"You'll get where you're supposed to go and be there when you're supposed to be there."

"You make it sound so simple, so easy."

"Well, Jenny Lee, most folks make a hard thing

out of life. It's already hard enough without trying to make it harder. I don't have ties, so I just take the road as it comes."

"But you keep moving. What are you looking for?"

Gunn cocked his head, drew a deep breath.

"Now," he said quietly, "you've asked a question I can't answer."

Jenny Lee knew she should have gone back to town with Willa. But she did not regret her decision to stay with Gunn. Tom Yire would not be back until late that night. Gunn was waiting until after dark before riding back into town. She knew it was sudden, but the man had affected her deeply in ways she didn't understand. Every time she was close to him, her skin tingled, her stomach tilted, filled with fluttering moths, and she had a strange stirring in her loins.

Now that the sun was settling over the far rimrock, softening the land, drenching it with shrill golds and filling up with ochre shadows, she felt a rare excitement as she finished the last touches on a pot of chili.

Smoked beef chunks simmered in a steaming stew of red beans laced with slivers of onions, shredded chili peppers, and just enough salt and masa flour to give it a sharp flavor and bulk. A gift from her mother, a fine cook. She wondered if Gunn could smell the chili, if it would please him. She wrapped flour tortillas in a dampened towl, set them in an iron bowl atop the stove to steam until they were warm. Tom kept a fair larder and she had enjoyed making supper while Gunn smoked outside.

She felt somewhat wicked fixing this meal for a man she had just met. The supper was a bribe. An invitation.

Jenny Lee Carter wanted Gunn.

She knew that now. She wanted him with all her heart. And she vowed to go to any lengths to get him.

There was time. It would not be full dark for two hours and supper was ready. She found a faded tablecloth, spread it on the wood table. She put a fresh candle in the candleholder, lit it. She set the plates close together, napkins beside them, then stepped back to survey her handiwork.

So rapt in her scheme was Jenny that she did not hear Gunn come up behind her.

"Smells mighty fine," he said.

"Oh!" Jenny jumped, turned, staggered into Gunn's arms. Her eyes widened as she looked up at him. So near, so tall.

"Didn't mean to scare you," he laughed, his arms around her to keep her from falling.

"I—I—you . . ." she stammered. "I—I didn't know you were here."

"Smelled the food."

"Hungry?"

"As a bear."

But Jenny did not move. She basked in the warmth of his arms. Gunn squeezed her and helped her stand straight.

"You all right?" he asked.

"I—I liked it there," she said, before she thought. Then she clamped her teeth together as if to bite her tongue for being so bold. "I mean . . . thank you for holding me up."

Her heart beat wildly in her chest and her breath whistled through her mouth. She could still feel his arms around her, the hard muscles of his arms holding her.

Gunn's mouth twisted in a puzzled smile.

"Jenny," he said softly, "you ought to have gone back into town with Willa."

"No," she said quickly. "I—I didn't want to . . . I wanted to stay here with you. Real bad, Gunn. Please don't make fun of me."

"I won't. But you just met me. You don't know anything about me."

"I know enough. Oh, I shouldn't speak so bold, I know, but you make me all giddy." She had told him of her life, but he had told her little. Now she wanted to know all about him. More than that, she wanted him to hold her again. Hold her and never let her go.

"First impressions can be wrong," he said.

"I don't care. Gunn, you won't hurry into town after supper, will you?"

"Why I ought to get in. Things should be set up by now and some men getting impatient wondering when the other's boot's going to fall."

"Please, stay with me awhile. You don't have to do anything. Just let me be near you, listen to you talk. Maybe hold me again."

Jenny's face flushed crimson and she bowed her head.

Gunn reached out, grabbed her hand. Squeezed it. Something about the young woman touched him.

She was all alone, an orphaned adult, trying to make her way in a hard land. He could understand that. Something about her reached out to him, a memory struggling for recognition, a fragment of himself as a young man buried for so long, suddenly emerging in her talk, her eyes.

"We don't have to eat right now," he said. "And we don't have to eat much. But you got to know I'll be riding on if I get out of this. I got to ride into Pima Flat to do some bad business."

Sparkles of light lit Jenny's eyes. Hope flashed on her face. She turned her hand, squeezed his tightly. Briefly.

"I want to go with you anywhere you go!" she blurted. "I—I'll help you! I'll cook for you, mend your clothes, make your bed. Oh, I just don't know if I can spend another minute in that hot dusty town with all those terrible men pawing over me."

"Jenny, Jenny," he soothed, "don't take on so. You can't go with me. Not yet. Maybe not ever . . ."

Impulsively, she rushed to him, threw her arms around his waist. She nudged her body hard against his. She mashed her breasts against his chest, thrust her thighs against his loins.

A hot flood of desire overpowered her as she trembled against his body. She grasped his arm, squeezed it, rubbed it frantically. The friction generated heat so that her palm became hot, as hot as if she had laid it on the stove.

Gunn felt heat flood his loins. The closeness of her, the scent from her hair, her touch, all conspired to stir his own desire.

"Jenny . . ." he husked.

"Gunn, I want you; want you so bad I'll do anything to make you want me too."

He reached down, tilted her head up. Bent to kiss her. Found her lips with his, slid his tongue inside her mouth. She crushed her lips against his in eager response. Her body melded to his and the heat spread through them, consuming them, blotting out all other senses.

She suckled his tongue, tried to swallow it.

Gunn's manhood swelled, rose up inside his trousers, pressed against her thigh.

She felt it pressing into her flesh, reached down, grasped it desperately, kneaded its swollen bulk with frantic fingers.

"Yes, yes," she gasped, breaking the kiss, "this is what I want, Gunn."

She released her grip on his cock, thrust her loins hard up against it, began rubbing the swollen member, her senses out of control, her desire complete. Cloth separated them, cheated them, yet heightened their lust for each other.

"Jenny," Gunn said, "it will be a damn sight easier if we get undressed."

"Yes . . ."

He grabbed her hand, led her from the kitchen, past the table and down the hall to the bedroom.

"The food," she said, "it'll . . ."

". . . keep . . ."

She floated behind him as he headed for the bedroom in long strides, dragging her along behind him. He charged through the door, entered the sparsely furnished bedroom.

Jenny began unbuttoning her blouse, unfastening

her skirt. Gunn didn't waste any time shucking his clothes. She emerged, seconds later, naked, her flesh soft as cream, her breasts jutting from her chest, the nipples hard as acorns. Gunn lifted her onto the bed, fell atop her. He took her in his arms, smothered her with his bulk, kissed her ravenously: her throat, her lips, her breasts, her nipples.

Jenny cried out with delight, her voice quavering with lunacy, desire.

He dove between her legs, nosed through the tangle of wiry pubic hairs, parted her lips with his tongue. He plumbed the pudding of her sex until she was clawing at his back, raking it with her fingernails. Her back arched, her loins pushed upward, taking him deeper. Her sex-cleft gushed with hot oils, her inner recesses ran with honey.

She drew her hands up his back, over his shoulders, threaded her fingers through his hair, clutched him as the first searing orgasm rippled through her flesh, growing in intensity until she screamed. Again and again, she screamed, her voice dulling against the adobe walls, streaming out the window into the gathering dusk. An animal cry of lust and triumph. The scream of a woman in the throes of fulfillment, gratification.

Gunn broke free and crawled her small frame, the lust in him fierce, hammering at his temples, burning his flesh, throbbing in the engorged veins of his manhood. Jenny's legs went wide and he burrowed into her, deep into her honeypot, ramming clear to the mouth of her womb until her scream rose up into a shrill high-pitched howl of pleasure.

Jenny bucked as orgasms laced her womb like

chain-lightning.

"Gunn, oh, Gunn . . . !" she screamed.

Gunn rose up on stiffened arms, looked down at her face and saw the raw passion in her eyes, on her wet lips and pulsing in her neck. He saw her and knew he was lost.

He saw her beauty and he saw the past he had forgotten. He saw her savage lust and her shameless desire.

And he saw Laurie for a brief instant and remembered how she had given herself to him in this way, given him everything, even her life.

"Jenny, Jenny," he breathed, and fell upon her, closing his eyes, drowning in her depths, melting in her heat.

Falling so far, from such a great height, he thought he might never come back up.

And he didn't care.

Maybe Jenny was the woman he had been looking for all these years.

Maybe . . .

CHAPTER TEN

Jed Randall swam in and out of consciousness.

The hard chair dug into his back. The way they had him braced, he could not move without sending the pain shooting through his shoulder. His arms were bent over the back of the chair, rope around his wrists, lashed to his legs on the underside.

Jason Coker sat close to him, holding that infernal cane.

"He's coming around again, Pa," said Randy Coker, sitting on the floor, his legs drawn up, crossed.

Jason nodded. He lifted the cane, held it like a cue stick.

"Randall? You hear me?"

Jed tried to focus. Coker's head bobbed like a balloon a few inches away, or a few miles . . .

"Yair," he said tightly, the effort sending pain through his shoulder again.

"See this cane?"

Randall's head cleared. He saw the cane. Remembered what Coker had been doing with it. Sweat broke out on his forehead, dripped into his eyes.

It all came back to him. Langley's quick shot. The bullet ripping into his shoulder, slamming him down against the counter, the floor turning slippery with his own blood. Voices. Yelling. Arms jerking him roughly to his feet. Coker and the others coming over from El Pozo Seco, dragging him roughly upstairs, lashing him to the chair. How long ago? An hour? Two? A few minutes?

Jed didn't know. He just knew that Coker was trying to break him down, make him spill his guts.

"Randall, you listening?" Jason said, leaning closer, the cane tip pointed at his shoulder. "Where's Gunn? I want him."

"You go plumb to hell, Coker!"

Coker shot the cane forward through his fingers. His aim was accurate. The cane-tip smashed into the open bullet wound.

Jed screamed.

Langley, standing next to him, stuffed a rag into Jed's mouth.

Coker shot the cane again and again into the wound, thumping the bullet hole with deadly accuracy. Randall's eyes widened in pain. His muffled screams fought to escape through the rag. The muscles and veins in his neck bulged against the flesh.

He got sick, vomited.

He strangled, turned blue in the face.

Coker jerked the rag out. Vomit gushed from Randall's mouth, down his chin and onto his bloody shirt.

He retched for several seconds, coughing and spluttering, fighting for air.

His eyes glazed.

Coker looked at him in disgust. The others in the room turned away. Some things a man didn't do to another man. But no one said anything. Coker was the boss. He was paying for their loyalty. Bat Hudson wanted a drink bad. He didn't hold much with torture. But Coker had told them all to stay. He was in a rage. Furious that Gunn wasn't there, that Randall wouldn't talk.

Paul Burns and Pete Cantwell seethed, but said nothing. They sat on the floor, too, their backs against the bed, wondering if their thirst would strangle them before Coker stopped working Randall over with a cane. At first, they were excited, smelling blood, but now that Coker had slowed things down they didn't like it. Randall wasn't the man they came for. He was wounded and could use a drink. Every time Coker hit that wound both men winced inwardly. No man ought to be used up like that. Like a damned dog or a gutshot buck.

These men were hard, but they had their own code. Randall had not drawn on anyone nor done any of them wrong. He was just the wrong man in the wrong place.

"We might of made a mistake," whispered Burns to Cantwell.

"Eh?"

"With Coker."

"Yeah."

Jason turned around quickly, his eyes glistening with hatred.

"Shut up, you two!" he ordered. "What the hell you jawin' about?"

Jack Martin, sprawled on the bed, shoved his hat back and hauled himself up on his elbows.

"Back off, Coker," he drawled, "we're all gettin' pretty sick of this shit."

Coker stiffened his back.

Randy twisted on the floor, hotheaded as a two-year bull.

Langley grinned. It was about time someone spoke up.

"You keep your mouth to yourself, Martin," Jason said. "You aren't getting paid for your opinions."

"No, well, Randy there hired us, but he said it was for killing a man. Not for stripping a man down like you're doing."

Jack swung a leg over the bed. His sudden movement caused Jason to stiffen. Jack moved the other leg, pushed himself up to a sitting position.

"You want to play hob with this man, Coker, fine. But I don't have to sit here and listen to him scream and puke all over hisself. I'm going over to the Pozo and get drunk."

Martin stood up, stood wide-legged facing Coker. The challenge was laid down.

Jason didn't avert his eyes from Martin, but stared him down, coldly, calmly.

Randy Coker didn't move, but his hand inched toward his holstered pistol.

Langley's smile froze on his face like pancake batter.

"You go on over there, Martin," said Coker evenly. "Anybody wants to go with you, can do the same. But it's on your own time. When you get your head straight, you come back and we'll talk about it."

"Fuck you, Coker," said Martin, dropping his

eyes. "Come on, Bat, you don't want to watch this shit either."

Bat Hudson got to his feet. The two men swaggered from the room. Langley made a move as if to go with them. Paul Burns sat still. Pete Cantwell fished the makings out of his vest pocket, ripped out a paper. The door slammed and it was quiet in the room.

Jason turned back to Randall, quivering inside with a deep rage that rolled like a savage sea.

"Cut him out of his trousers," he ordered Langley.

Langley blinked, drew his blade.

He hesitated.

"Cut 'em off," said Jason.

Langley loosened Randall's belt, drew it from its loops, tossed it to the floor like a dead snake. He pulled on the waistband of the bound man's trousers and began slicing downward clear to the cuff on one side. He did the same with the other and jerked the pants free.

"The shorts too," said Coker.

Langley shrugged, cut away Randall's undershorts.

Randall seemed to shrink in the chair.

Langley stepped away, as Burns and Cantwell stretched forward to see what Coker would do next.

What Coker did next was to pull a cigar from his shirt pocket, bite the tip off and spit it in Randall's face. Then he struck a sulphur match, lit the cigar end, and blew smoke into Randall's eyes at close range.

Jed's eyes filled with tears. He gagged on the foul

smoke, straining against his bonds.

Randy Coker looked at his father with glittering eyes, transfixed on this casual demonstration of cruelty. He licked his lips, rocked forward and stretched his mouth in a demented smile. This was something he could understand; this was hatred turned to action, subtle as the snick of a knife blade in a dark alley.

Jason pulled on the cigar until the tip was glowing like cherry coals. Then, abruptly, he jabbed the cigar into the pulpy soft flesh of one of Randall's testicles.

Randall screamed as his flesh started to burn, as blue smoke curled up in the air, acrid with the taint of singed hair. Langley clamped a hand over Randall's mouth. Randy Coker leaped to his feet, snatched up the rag. Langley withdrew his hand; Randy stuffed the rag in Jed's mouth.

"Now, Randall," said Jason, "you just nod when you're ready to talk and we'll take the gag out."

Jed's eyes seemed about to burst from their sockets as he strangled on his own screams. His face turned purple, the cords in his neck stood out like whip welts. Still, he did not give in to Coker, but held on, the pain driving through him like a fiery knife ripping upward from his crotch to his brain.

Coker sucked on the cigar again, pulling air through it until the tip once more began to glow like a smithy's furnace. Jed watched him with horror-stricken eyes, his left testicle throbbing so hard he felt it in his temples. He didn't know if he could take it any more. The resolve he had built up in himself softened like lead in a hot-pot. He was stripped of his dignity and now the torture had weakened him further. How long could he hold out? And what if he told them where Gunn was? Would they stop now? A man like Coker had something twisted inside him. He was like an animal and there was no reasoning with him.

Coker brought the cigar down from his mouth, sailed it slowly toward Randall's exposed genitals.

Jed watched the moving cigar in stark horror.

He wanted to scream, to kick, to disappear. Yet he was helpless, bound to the chair like a trussed goose. There was no escape. He had to talk or Coker would turn him into something he loathed even more than pain: a groveling coward, willing to say anything to get off the hook. But maybe that was the answer. Tell Coker what he wanted to know, except avoid the truth so that Gunn would not suffer from his own weakness.

As the cigar tip drew close to his scrotum, Jed felt the heat from its glow. In a second or two, the tip would touch his bare flesh and he would scream through his gag. Or pass out.

Randall began nodding his head vigorously. Muffled noises issued from the gag in his mouth.

Coker stopped the cigar as it singed a straggled hair on Jed's sac.

"Take out his gag," Coker ordered. Langley pulled it free and Jed sucked in air.

"You ready to tell us where Gunn is?"

"Yes, godammit."

"You'd better talk fast and talk straight, Randall, or I'll ram this cigar up your asshole."

Coker's face was a mask of finality.

Randall believed him.

"All—all right," he gasped. "He—he's hiding out. Till morning. I don't know exactly where, but . . ."

Savagely, Coker drove the hot cigar into Randall's unburnt testicle.

Randall rose up in the chair, slamming into the ropes. The front chair legs lifted a good four inches from the floor. The chair came back down with a crash as Randall bit his lips to keep from screaming. Blood oozed from the tender flesh, tasted salty in his mouth. Lights burst like fireworks in his brain and the pain rose up in his throat like a mailed fist.

"Jesus!"

"You keep lyin' to me, Randall, holdin' back, you'll be talkin' in a high-pitched voice. Permanent."

Randall groped for an answer. A good answer. One that would satisfy Coker and keep his own manhood intact. But even a lie would be trouble. Somewhere down the line. Someone would get hurt. The wrong people could get hurt. Yet Gunn might be caught unawares if Coker really knew where he was. He might be shot down without a chance. Time. He needed time. Needed time for himself, for Gunn. Get Coker moving. Get him hot on a cold trail. Get him away from his balls with that burning cigar.

"Hidin' out at the Lazy L," Randall gasped, shocked by the enormity of his own lie. "Got sweet on that turnip out there and rode on back soon as he saw you had him outnumbered."

Coker sucked in a breath. He rammed his face close to Randall's, peered into his eyes.

"If you're lying, Randall, I'll drag you clear to the

Lazy L on your belly."

Jed almost burst out laughing.

Coker was buying it! Lock, stock and barrel full of bullshit.

"No lie, Coker. Jesus, would I lie? You got me cold. Gunn rode on back, said he'd be here in the morning. Couldn't keep it in his pants. One last time he told me, just in case he died. But he made me swear not to tell, and now I'm sick as hell you got it out of me."

Was he laying it on too thick? Jed knew he had talked fast, but something in Coker's eyes made him see that it was being swallowed. That touch about the gal. Inspired. But what would happen when Coker found out Gunn wasn't there? All hell would break loose and his own life wasn't worth a tinker's dam. Well, it wasn't worth a good goddamn, now, either. Coker had him, literally, by the balls.

Randy Coker rose to his feet. His face was livid with rage.

"That sumbitch," he croaked. "I had that filly staked out for myself! I'll kill the bastard. I'll blow his fuckin' balls off!"

"Shut the hell up, Randolph," said his father. "Didn't I tell you? Gunn can't keep his hands off the women."

Randy backed off, chastened. Whenever his father used his given name it hurt. He didn't like the name. It was too high-toned. He still didn't like the idea of Gunn going after a woman he had cut out of the herd.

Jed Randall quivered inside. He wanted to let out his breath in a sigh of relief, but it was too soon.

But Coker had bought it!

As if reading his thoughts, Jason Coker said: "You're not out of it yet, Randall! Gunn may be out at the Lazy L and he may not. If he isn't you're going to be squeak-voiced as a meadowlark. Savvy? I mean I'll geld you with a dull knife if I find out you lied to me."

"He's out there," said Randall, a touch of defiance in his voice. *Nail it down. Don't let Coker know just yet. Time. Time for Gunn to get to town. Time for his life to be saved. Time to hold onto the family jewels.*

Coker looked at Randall for a long time. Then, grunting, he stood up, leaning on his cane.

He looked at his son.

"Randy, how long would it take you and Langley to ride out to Lassiter's?"

"Two hours goin', two back."

"It'll be dark."

"I know the way." Randy straightened, lifted his chin proudly.

"You be back here before midnight. No foolin' around with that gal. If Gunn's there, you leave Langley there and come back. I want to be there for the kill."

"And if he ain't there?" drawled Langley.

Coker flashed a hard look at Jed.

"Then you both hightail it back here. We'll give Randall here a drag party at the end of a rope."

Langley grinned, nodded.

"Come on," said Randy, "let's get to it."

After they had left, Jason looked at Randall for a long time. Jed's head hung over his chest, his breathing shallow. Every so often he twitched in pain.

"Get this bastard out of here," he told Burns. "Put him in his own room and keep him tied fast. You sit there and shoot anyone who tries to get him free. We want you, we'll knock three times."

Burns nodded, walked over to Randall.

"Cantwell, you stay here. I'm going down to the Elk's Head to get a bottle. I've been in this damned room too long."

Jed Randall tried to stand, once his bonds were loosened, but the feeling had gone out of his legs. He watched Jason Coker limp to the door and leave.

Paul Burns reluctantly helped Randall to stand.

"You'd better pray real hard, feller," he said to Randall, "this this Gunn jasper is out at that ranch. Else you'll be wolf meat afore morning. Coker means business."

"Yeah," said Randall, "well maybe Coker's doing a little praying himself. He and Gunn have been at this before and you know what happened."

"Shut up!" said Cantwell, an edginess to his voice. "Paul, get his ass out of here."

Randall managed a smile. He had struck bone. And, he was still alive.

CHAPTER ELEVEN

T.O. Lassiter rose out of bed dripping with sweat. The pain had subsided, soaked in brandy, dulled by a lull in his body's invasion of alien, malformed cells.

This was not the way for a man to go. Not when he still had a spark of life left in him. This was not the way he wanted to go.

It was dark inside the room, dark outside. Cool. Cool enough to feel the fever burning his face like a hot southwest wind. Esmerelda must have retired. It had been quiet in the house for a long time. He had sipped the brandy for the better part of an hour, letting it trickle down his throat and into his raw belly until he was lightheaded enough to think straight.

Gunn had gone into Pima Flat to face a group of killers who outnumbered him. Maybe his friend Randall would be able to help him, maybe not. But Gunn could use all the help he could get. Even help from a dying man.

T.O. slid off the bed, found his boots on the dark floor. Odd, now that he had made his decision, he felt better. Stimulated. The pain was there, but it was not gut-wrenching.

It took him a long time to find what he needed—the gunbelt and pistol, check its loads. He kept sipping the brandy, ramming the bottle inside his shirt as he went outside to saddle up. He told himself he wasn't drinking for courage, but only to keep the pain in check.

He got out his tack, caught up a good horse, saddled her. A sorrel mare that would not spook at shadows. That was important. He had to stay in the saddle. He had to get to Pima Flat and side with Gunn. That was a better way of dying than this way, burning up inside, being eaten alive by some kind of devilish tapeworm that lived in his guts.

"Pa, what are you doing?"

T.O. turned, startled. He hadn't heard his daughter come up.

"L.D., leave me be," he said.

She stood in the shadowy moonlight, a wraithlike figure in her gown, rifle cradled in her arms.

She lay the rifle down, rushed to him. He had just finished tightening the last cinch. She threw her arms around him, squeezed him until his breath caught. He felt a wetness on his cheek where her face rubbed his and knew she was crying.

"Pa, you can't do this. Please. Don't leave me. If you go I'll never see you again."

Gently, he pried her arms from his waist, tried to see her face clearly in the shadows. The horses nickered restlessly in the corrals, their sleep disturbed.

"Listen, girl," he said tightly, "I got to go. My last chance to do somethin' good for a friend."

"It isn't that, Pa. You're drinking. Give me that bottle." She had felt it when she squeezed him, mashing her midriff. "We can talk about this in the morning. When your head is clear. Let me put you back to bed, take care of you."

T.O. backed away from his daughter, defensively.

"No, L.D. NO! Don't try to stop me. I don't want to die in that dadgummed bed! Let me go out like a man. If you care for me, you'll step aside and let me ride in for a friend's sake."

"For Gunn," she whispered, startled at her father's vehemence.

"Yes. For Gunn. For me. For you."

"You're not drunk, are you? I mean not really."

"No. Just tired of the pain. Tired of hiding it from myself."

She could sense the pain. It sang off his teeth, hissed through his mouth. She could feel it now, inside herself. Suddenly, she was very sad. And confused. It was hard to understand. Not her father's going, but death itself. It was so close now she could smell it, taste it. She shrank back away from it, stunned by its lizardy dankness, its ravishing chill.

"Pa, how can I just . . . just let you go?"

Softened, T.O. stepped towards her, wanting to take her in his arms. He removed the bottle from his shirt, set it on the ground. He hugged her tightly, lay her head on his shoulder.

"If a man is responsible for his own life," he said, quietly, "then he's got to be responsible for his death too. If he can. I don't have much time left. I don't want you to see me waste away, turn into a sniveling pup. I don't want to scream when the pain gets too bad and have you hear me and end up hating me for making your own life miserable. That's what happens, child, when a man gets old and sick and can't take care of himself anymore. He just turns into a squalling baby, shitting his pants and pissing in his bed."

"Pa . . ."

"No, you got to hear it. I got to get it out. I thought this out long ago. Long before you came back. I hoped it would come some other way. Get bit by a snake or fall off my horse and break my head. Get caught in a flash flood and just keep on going till I ran out of breath. Or just drop over dead peaceful as a stone. But now the pain in my gut gnaws at me. It clogs up my brain. I just got to go my own way, with my boots on."

"You want them to shoot you!"

"No, L.D. I'm just going to side a man who's outnumbered. I'd do it anyway, probably, but I'm doing it now because that bed was like a damned coffin with the lid up and everybody looking in at me. A man ought to be able to pick not only how he dies, but where he dies. I'll do mine standing up if I can."

T.O.'s effort drained him of energy. Made him sweat until he smelled the sourness of it rising up from his soaked shirt. It was time to go. If he didn't leave now, he'd never make it. The pain was back, grinding his insides up with chili peppers.

He stepped away from his daughter, stooped for the bottle. Fearsome pain shot through his bowels. Lye poured into a raw wound. He cursed under his breath, straightened up. The horse swam before his eyes. He hauled himself up into the saddle, sat there, reeling, groggy.

"You stay here, L.D. Watch the place for me. For both of us. If I don't come back, you look in the strongbox under the loose slat in my bedroom. You'll get by."

"Pa . . ."

"Hush now. Maybe it'll be Gunn who rides back instead of me. Or maybe we'll both ride back together. This might be the medicine I need."

L.D. choked back the tears. There was so much she wanted to say to her father. The words wouldn't form. They floated in her mind, out of reach, like vagrant balloons. And then T.O. was riding away, into the night, down the road with the dust rising up behind him, blotting him out until there was only the sound of the horse's hooves rattling loose stones and thumping on the ground. Finally, there was just an emptiness and she didn't know if it was on the road or inside herself.

Gunn knew he should be moving, riding out, but Jenny Lee was beneath him and he was inside her. That was all that mattered. The pleasures of the flesh. Fleeting pleasures at that. With this one and that one. But this one was different. Oh yes? Maybe. Different enough. A softness inside her like iron. Like an iron spider web. Sticky. And he the fly.

She made sounds with her mouth. Good sounds, like a dove cooing, a cat purring, or a breeze soaring over a marshland. And cried out when he sank deep inside the moist hot folds of her flesh.

He kissed her again, unable to resist that swollen mouth of hers, the yielding lips, the firm tongue.

His hand kneaded her breast again. The right one. Tender as a mushroom. In the dark she was a child, her sex tight on his manhood, squeezing him like a delicate handshake. Her loins quivering with passion, her sex-cleft squeezing him, drawing him deeper somehow, into the dank, the heat, the endless tunnel of mystery.

"Gunn, I—I've come a hundred times."

"Dozens."

"But you, how can you stand it so long?"

"I can't," he breathed, stroking her, plumbing that endless dark depth that was like a night river in a dream.

"You don't have to hold back. I'm satisfied."

Yes, he thought, *but I'm not. I don't want it to end. I don't want to die inside her and then have to get up and leave her while I go into town and shoot men dead.*

He didn't say anything.

Jenny Lee moved her hips, jutted her sex up so that he plumbed her even deeper. She wriggled and he held fast inside her, blocking out the desire that welled up in him. He could let it go now. Let all of it go and it would be over. Maybe forever. He might never see Jenny Lee Carter again. Might never feel this way with any other woman. Coker could kill him. Or one of his men. His son, his slackmouthed brat.

Hold on, hold on until the last possible minute. Until Jenny Lee screamed again. Until she clawed his back to shreds and clamped her legs around him in a spasmic seizure.

He could hold on no longer, finally.

Jenny skewered him into herself and he could no longer block the urgency of his own desire.

Jenny misted into Laurie and then he was lost.

She pulled him down, held him until his seed burst free from its sac. He held on to her, spewing his sperm, splashing it into her like a hurled bucket full of whitewash. She gasped, clawed, squirmed. Gunn trembled, died the little death.

"Jenny!" he cried out, and to his surprise, it was Jenny beneath him. Not Laurie. "Oh, Jenny!"

She held him tight until his spasms passed. Until the limpness was complete.

"Oh, Gunn. Oh Gunn!" she whispered, her hands suddenly tender again, clawless.

Jason Coker limped to the table in the Elk's Head.

Quiet, shadow-faced men drank in solitary clusters at other tables, at the bar. Ranchers, drovers, drifters off the main trail. The women could not be seen at all. Not their faces. Only their skirts, an arm, a patch of glowing hair in the lamplight.

Tom Yire sent a girl over to Coker's table.

"Whiskey," he gruffed.

"Want me to sit with you?"

"No, bring the bottle."

Jason heard the girl whispering, shot her a glance. He did not know her name, but he sensed that she was talking about him, to the bartender. The bartender looked at him, turned away quickly.

Coker's brain teemed with warning signals.

"You, gal," he said loudly. "Come here."

"Me?" asked Willa.

Tom Yire nudged her with his finger, nodded in

Coker's direction.

Willa came over, but slowly, as if afraid.

"Sit down," said Coker. "Want to talk to you."

Willa sat down, whitefaced, nervous.

"What do you want to talk about?"

"You know Randall?"

"Yes."

"Seen him lately?"

"Not since . . . since he was shot."

"Well, he's all right. Just a flesh wound. You fancy him?"

"Some, yes."

"Some, huh? You know his pard, Gunn?"

"No," she said quickly. Too quickly.

Coker's hand snaked out, grabbed her arm. His face turned to stone.

"You know him! You seen him! I want to know where!"

"Please, sir, you're hurting me!"

"I'll break your arm if you don't tell me where you saw this Gunn last."

Coker kept his voice low, but his fingers dug into Willa's arm. He saw the fear in her eyes, smelled it. He drew her close so she could see that he meant business.

"He—he's staying at Tom's—the bartender's. What have you done with Jed?"

Coker released Willa's arm, his breathing heavy.

"Tell Tom to come over here," he husked.

Willa scrambled to her feet, nearly ran into the girl bringing the bottle and glass to Coker's table. She rushed over to the bar, whispered to Tom Yire. Yire shook his head as Coker watched him. Coker beckoned to him with a single finger. Coker poured a drink, drank half of it from the shot glass as Tom made his way around the bar, headed for the table. He stopped at two tables along the way.

"Mister Coker," said Yire, taking the initiative, "you better leave. We don't manhandle women here. There's at least four guns trained on you right now. If you so much as move your gun arm, you'll be shot."

Coker looked beyond Yire at the other tables between him and the bar. Men stared at him, their hands under the table.

"Goddamn you, man, you'll regret this."

"Get out," said Yire. "And stay out."

Coker got to his feet, his face flushed with anger. He said nothing more, but limped toward the lobby, his cane coming down hard on the wood flooring.

Tom Yire breathed out.

He looked over his shoulder at Willa, who was standing at the bar.

Her face was chalk.

He walked to her, found that his hands were shaking.

"I'm going to find Gunn," he told her. "Tell Larry to watch the bar. Coker didn't look none too happy."

"Tom," she said, "be careful. That man is dangerous."

He knew. And the shaking wouldn't stop.

Jason knocked on Pete Cantwell's door.

"Who is it?"

"Coker. Open up."

Paul Burns opened the door. Pete Cantwell had his pistol out. Jed Randall lay on the floor, trussed and gagged.

"What's up, boss?" asked Burns.

"We've been doublecrossed. Get Randall on his feet. Tie his hands behind his back, leave him gagged."

Cantwell cut the leg bonds, jerked Randall upright. His hands were already tied fast behind his back.

"Come on, we'll saddle up," said Coker.

"Where we goin'?" asked Burns.

"To drag this sonofabitch until he tells us where that bartender lives."

Randall glared at Coker. Coker stepped up to him, jerked the gag out of his mouth.

"One last chance, Randall. I know Gunn is holed up. Question is, where? You show, us, you live."

"Fuck you, Coker."

They had put pants on Randall. They fit badly, but at least he had some dignity left. Coker, he now knew, would kill him anyway. Once he told. He wondered how he had found out where Gunn was. Apparently he didn't know where Tom Yire lived and that could only mean that it hadn't been Yire who told him. Willa? Probably. But obviously she had not given Coker directions. Something had happened. Coker was boiling mad. Killing mad.

"We'll see how you feel after running against a cactus or two," said Coker.

The three men prodded Randall ahead of them as they walked down the hall, out through the lobby downstairs. The clerk looked up, said nothing.

They saddled three horses at the livery.

Cantwell unlimbered a manila rope. He looped it under Randall's wrist bonds, tightened it down.

Then, Cantwell tied the bitter end to his saddle horn.

The men rode out the back of the stable, into the hazy night. Randall walked after them, still upright. They rode slow until they cleared the town.

"Head toward the Lazy L," said Coker. "We'll likely run into Randy and Langley on their way back to town. Kick 'em out, boys!"

Cantwell dug his spurs into his horse's flanks.

The horse bolted.

Jed walked faster, then ran. He ran until his legs jerked out from under him. He hit the ground hard, felt the breath explode out of him.

CHAPTER TWELVE

Gunn tied Esquire up to the hitching rail across the street from the hotel, a few doors down from El Pozo Seco.

Most of the street was dark, but light spilled out from the Pozo, the Elk's Head and the San Carlos Hotel, stained the dusty street a coppery yellow-bronze. A dog's silhouette appeared down the street, then disappeared into ghostly shadows. A bat streaked overhead on silent wings, knifing through the still air with tiny bloodied teeth.

Jenny Lee was still at Yire's, and now he wished he had brought her with him. A half hour ago, he had almost been run down by Yire himself. Going out to warn him. Coker knew and was blood-mad, according to Tom. Well, now Yire could get Jenny, sneak her back to town, keep her safe until this business was over. Coker would not hesitate to kill them both if he knew they had given Gunn shelter. The man seemed even more deranged than before he had gone to prison—if that was possible.

He had stayed too long at Yire's. Eaten burnt tortillas and stew, mooning over Jenny by candlelight.

Tempted to stay another hour at that. Forget about Coker and his mad vendetta. Just grab the woman and keep riding. But reason had prevailed and he had to push Jenny out of his mind for the time being. Until Coker was put away in a pine box under six feet of Arizona dirt.

Gunn crossed the street in a few easy strides. He looked at the light in the hotel lobby for a long time before he went inside. The lobby, he noted, was empty. The clerk looked up from a game of solitaire as Gunn leaned over the counter.

"Jason Coker upstairs?"

"Left a good half hour ago. Him and Cantwell, Burns."

The names meant nothing to Gunn.

"What about his whelp, Randy?"

"He left earlier'n that, with that other feller, Langley."

Another unknown name.

"Any of his men upstairs?"

The clerk licked dry lips, hesitated.

"I mean to find out," said Gunn. "One way or the other."

"Hudson and Martin went to the Pozo, I think. Say, Mister, you ask a lot of questions."

"If Coker comes in, tell him I took his room. Now I'll have his key."

"You're the second feller asked for that room. First one got shot. Randall."

Gunn's mouth filled with a sour taste. He felt a sinking in his stomach as if the floor had dropped out from under him.

"Jed Randall?"

"Yep. Been quite a busy night. Langley shot him, from that chair over yonder."

The clerk stood up, pointed to the chair in the corner. Bathed in yellow lamp light. Gunn looked down, saw dried brown stains on the wood floor.

"Did Langley kill him?" Gunn asked, his throat suddenly dry as a bone.

"Nope. Randall walked out of here with Mister Coker a half hour ago."

"Huh?"

"He didn't look none too good, but it was him all right."

"Where'd they go?"

"The livery. Oh, I keep my eyes open."

"Yeah," said Gunn drily. "I'll have that key."

"Can't do that, Mister. Against the rules."

Gunn didn't want to waste any more time with him. But he needed a room. Someplace to wait if he had to.

"Give me another room, then," he said.

"Full up."

"I'll take your room then. You won't need it anymore."

"How come?"

"You're going to a funeral."

"No! Whose?"

"Yours, friend, if you don't have a room ready and a key for me when I get back."

"Well, you put it that way, I got a room. Name?"

"Gunn."

The clerk started to shake all over. His trembling hands pulled a key from a dusty cubbyhole.

"Small room, hardly used. At the end of the hall.

Number 18."

Gunn took the key, ignored the ledger the clerk shoved toward him.

"Two dollars."

Gunn peeled off two one-dollar bills, pocketed the key.

"You say two of Coker's men are at the cantina across the street?"

"They went there. I don't see everything what goes on."

Gunn turned away from the clerk, glanced at the doorway that led to the Elk's Head. A pair of men wobbled his way. He tensed, but they walked by him, upstairs. They were likkered up cowhands from the looks of them. Neither was armed.

Gunn walked outside, crossed the street. He could feel the clerk's eyes on him. A busybody. But he had gotten some useful information from him. Randall had been shot, but was still alive. Where had Coker taken him? And where had Randy and Langley gone? Nothing made sense. Maybe Jed was leading Coker on a wild goose chase. He hadn't counted on Coker's man shooting Jed. He owed Jed one for that.

Now, all bets were off. He had no plan. Just take them out one by one. Two across the street, the others out somewhere, looking for him most likely. At least he had seen no one between town and Yire's. Tom could get Jenny out. The only other place they could be was somewhere in town, or . . ."

Lassiter's!

Again, Gunn's stomach dropped four inches. T.O. was dying out there, and L.D. was by herself. If

Coker harmed her . . .

Men's voices drifted through the doors of El Pozo Seco. Gunn braced himself, again looked at the light before he went in. He heard the liquid Spanish speech mingled with the coarse American as he stepped inside. The bar was at the left, tables scattered to the right. A small, dark place. A pair of guitars leaned against chairs in one corner.

Heads turned. Talk died away.

Gunn strode to the bar, went to the far end, near the back entrance. It was a plain move and he knew Coker's men would read it right. A man scraped his chair on the dirt floor as he turned it to face the bar. The bartender, a small round Mexican wearing a dirty white apron came to the end of the bar.

He said nothing.

"You got any decent whiskey here?"

"*Si.* The best. American whiskey. One dollar."

"Set it out."

Some talk started up, but two men at one table just continued staring at him. The other men at the bar moved away from him, an inch at a time as if not wishing to cause offense. But they wanted to get out of the way. These were old timers and they could smell trouble a mile away. Two Mexicans got up quickly and left.

The bartender brought a bottle and a water glass. Gunn poured the glass a quarter full, raised it to his lips. He nodded in the direction of the two men who watched him intently.

"Here's to Jason Coker," he said loudly, plunking a cartwheel on the bar, "and to his friends."

Bat Hudson jerked as Jack Martin jabbed an

elbow in his side. Both men were staring at the stranger but neither could believe his ears.

"You hear that, Bat?"

"Yair, I heard. Shut up, Jack."

Bat's right hand inched off the table, came to rest on his holster.

"Who are you, stranger? You know Coker?"

"I know him," said Gunn.

Now the room was quiet. And everyone was staring at Gunn. But the two men at the table by the window were staring harder than anyone else.

"What was that toast again?"

Gunn smiled.

"I said, 'here's to Jason Coker; may his black heart rot in hell.' "

"Jesus," said Jack Martin. "Bat, that's . . ."

Bat ignored Martin.

"I asked your name, stranger," said Hudson.

"The name's Gunn. And yours?"

"Hudson. Bat Hudson."

Martin's hand started to move. Gunn stood slightly away from the bar, his right arm dangling. His left hand held the water glass.

"Then the feller next to you would be Martin. I hear you're looking for me."

"You heard wrong," said Hudson.

"I think you're a lying polecat," said Gunn evenly, his voice like a whip through the room. Strong words anywhere on earth, stronger here, now.

The silence thickened.

"Don't call him out, Bat," whispered Martin. "You know what Coker said."

"Shut up, Jack, dammit!"

Out of the corner of his eye, Gunn saw the bartender fall to the dirt floor, huddle under a counter.

Men moved toward the walls, clearing a path between Gunn and Coker's men. They moved slowly, but they moved.

Gunn wondered which one would go for it. He looked at their eyes, their shoulders. Martin froze, mouth open. Bat licked his lips. He'd be the one. Gunn would bet on it. But would Martin back his partner up? There was no way of telling. The distance between them seemed to shorten as the tension in the room built up like electrical clouds in a thunderstorm.

Martin dropped his eyes.

It would be Hudson, then.

Gunn stood his ground, waited.

Bat Hudson went for it.

He kicked away from the table, half-stood in a crouch, snaked his pistol from its holster.

Gunn almost admired his speed. But there wasn't time for that.

Sometimes you could let a man have the first shot. If he was in a hurry, nine times out of ten, he'd miss. His shot would go wild and then his advantage was gone.

In this case, Gunn didn't take chances.

His hand streaked for his Colt, snatched it free, cocked it in a single smooth motion. All this while stepping back a half foot so he'd have a clear field of fire. He pulled the trigger as soon as the pistol was level out of the holster. That shortened his draw time considerably. Hudson wasn't ready for that. Bat drew his pistol up, thumbed the hammer back and prepared to fire.

Gunn saw the surprise on Hudson's face as his own Colt barked. Hudson was still hammering back when the .45 slug caught him in the gut, just above his belt buckle.

Hudson staggered, half-turned by the impact of the bullet.

Through glazed eyes, he saw Gunn reappear through the swirl of white smoke.

Bat brought his pistol up, finished cocking it. He swung it to bear on Gunn. Gunn's pistol clicked as he hammered back, fired again. This time, Gunn took aim. A small blue hole appeared in Hudson's forehead. The back of his head flew apart. A pink spray spattered the window, the wall, the crown of Martin's hat. Hudson's mouth opened in an O of surprise and then his legs went out from under him. A foul stench filled the room as Hudson's sphincter muscle loosened. He fell in a heap, lay still as stone.

Jack Martin stood up, knees slightly bent, torso leaning forward.

Gunn's hammer.

Had it *clicked* again?

Martin wasn't sure. He stood there, arms handling like ape's arms. Wondering if he should go for it.

Gunn saw the man's hesitation.

He eased the hammer back down, holstered his pistol.

"Well," he said, looking at Martin, "same odds. You want to buy in?"

Jack let out a breath, shook his head.

"Nope," he said. "I like to pick my own time, Mister. And place. I'll pass."

"Suit yourself, Martin. I'll give you some friendly advice though."

"Yeah?"

"I got no quarrel with you. Only with Coker. You can ride on out of here, no one the wiser. We meet again, we can have a drink together. Coker won't be able to meet his payroll much longer if you're in his pay."

"I—I'll give it some serious thought."

"You do that, Martin."

Martin stepped away from the table. He edged toward the door, turned and walked slowly through it. The batwing doors creaked as they swung to a stop. No one in the room moved. They stared at Gunn.

Gunn still stood there, looking at the doors.

Then, he smiled.

"Drink up, boys," he said. "Party's over."

Conversation started up again. Still, Gunn stood there, facing the doors. Listening. Looking. Later, men would swear he was counting. To himself. The bartender stood up again, peered cautiously over the bar. Men drank, glasses clinked. No one made a move toward Hudson's body, and the stink still filled the air.

Gunn took two steps to his left, went into a crouch.

Before anyone knew what was happening, he drew his pistol again, cocked it.

The batwing doors burst open.

Jack Martin barreled through them, pistol in hand. The pistol bucked and orange flame belched from its barrel. Men dove for the floor.

Martin got off two quick shots. A picture shattered on the wall, a *mezcal* bottle exploded. All in the line of fire, on a direct path where Gunn had stood seconds before.

Gunn squeezed the trigger. His Colt boomed in his hand.

The bullet caught Martin in the right breast, plowed through ribs and muscle, tissue and lung. The hammering impact drove him to his left, staggered him against a table where the two men who had left had been sitting. He went down in a crash. His pistol skittered through the dust of the floor, spun twice and stopped.

Blood gushed from Martin's chest.

Gunn walked over, stood looking down at the dying man.

Martin looked up at him with glazed eyes. Pain twisted his facial muscles.

"Damn you!" he cursed.

Gunn ejected the empty hulls from the Colt. He shoved in fresh bullets, closed the gate on the cylinder. He spun the pistol over his trigger finger, let it fall easily into the holster.

"You're not so good at picking the time and place, Martin."

"Jesus," said Martin, before choking on a clot of blood.

Some of the Mexicans started crossing themselves.

Gunn looked at Martin one last time.

"Maybe he can help you," he muttered.

Gunn walked across the street, ignoring the people gathered outside the Elk's Head. He went into the hotel, suddenly weary.

"Coker come back?" he asked the clerk, who looked at Gunn in abject awe.

"My god, did you kill those two hardcases?"

"They died."

"Mister, you'll be famous. We saw Martin wait outside to get you. They were taking bets next door."

"Who was the favorite?"

"Why, Martin. No one figgered you had a chance."

"Too bad. I'd liked to have had a little of that easy money."

The clerk coughed. It was obvious he had bet on the wrong man, too.

"Mister, they ain't through. You still got five men to face down. They're saying you won't last until sundown tomorrow."

Gunn dug in his pocket, handed the clerk a twenty.

"Get the best odds, put me down for a double saw."

"On yourself?"

"Yeah, and now I'll trade you that small room for Hudson's."

"Give me a half hour to have it cleaned, Mister Gunn. You can have a drink at the Elk's Head. On the house." The clerk cackled, gave Gunn a wooden nickel good for a free drink.

It was the best offer he'd had since hitting town again.

CHAPTER THIRTEEN

T.O. Lassiter felt better after his third swig from the bottle. The rocking motion in the saddle kept his mind off the pain. It was better to be on a horse than in that damned sweaty bed. Under the stars, the moon, out in the dark where he felt at home, in his element. Coyotes barked in the hills, bats flicked through the air, emitting high-pitched squeaks, quail ticked warnings as his horse passed their nightbed. The moon was hidden behind high thin clouds and he liked it that way. His head was clear, the pain receding, bathed in booze.

The fourth time he stopped to take a swig from the bottle, he heard it.

Hoofbeats coming his way.

One, two miles away. Maybe more. Sounds carried far on the night air.

He slipped the bottle into the saddle bag, drew his pistol. Someone was sure as hell coming his way. Could be Gunn. Or trouble from town. He had been riding near an hour. Another hour to town. No one else settled out this way.

He listened carefully. At least two horses. The

sound faded, then sounded closer.

Lassiter urged his horse off the road, up into the shelter of saguaros, mesquite. He moved toward the sound, though, closing the gap.

Ten minutes later, he saw them. Two riders, coming at a steady pace, their horses loping just short of a gallop.

Lassiter reined in, waited.

In another four or five minutes, they'd be in range.

They loomed up out of the darkness. Lassiter hammered back, swung his horse around to his left.

"Hold up there!" he called.

The two horses skidded to a stop. Dust swirled. Pebbles bounced. Then it was quiet.

"Gunn? Is that you?"

Lassiter recognized the voice.

Randy Coker.

But who was the other man? Tall and lean, he held his horse behind Randy's so that Lassiter couldn't see him clearly. The men were twenty yards away.

"Lassiter," he said. "Gunn ain't here."

He heard the men whispering.

"He out at your place?" asked Randy.

"Nope. Goin' in to town to see him myself."

Then, before Lassiter knew what was happening he heard the other man slap his horse's rump.

"You'll play hell!" yelled Langley, bolting into the open, brandishing a rifle. Flame bloomed from the barrel and Lassiter heard the sizzle of a bullet frying the air.

His own pistol barked and bucked in his hand.

But his aim was high and wide. His horse jumped

at the sudden explosion, and Lassiter lurched almost out of the saddle.

"Don't shoot him!" yelled Randy.

Langley, ignoring the youth, charged straight at Lassiter, levering another round into the rifle's chamber. He fired again, ten yards away. Virtually pointblank range.

T.O. felt the slug smack into his side. The impact threatened to tear him from the saddle. He held on, grimly, swung his pistol on Langley. He couldn't see the man, but he saw his horse's heaving chest. He squeezed the trigger, felt the pistol butt slam into his palm.

Langley's horse went down, chest-shot. Langley himself went flying over the withers like a scarecrow caught in a whirlwind. He landed with a thud, cracking his head against a rock. His horse tried to get up, but blood gushed from the hole in its chest. Pink froth formed on its mouth, flecked the bit. It struggled to its haunches, wheezed in pain as Lassiter rode on by, hanging on to the saddle horn.

Randy saw Langley go down, thought he was hit.

Seconds later, Lassiter's horse shot by, hooves flying. Randy fired, but he was way behind in his lead. Turned the wrong way. He cursed, spurred his horse over to where Langley lay.

"Langley? Slicker?"

No answer.

Precious seconds ticked by. Randy dismounted, ground-tied his horse to a mesquite bush. His heart was thrumming in his chest, his throat knotted up. Something had gone wrong. It was confusing. What in hell was Lassiter doing out this late? And where in hell was Gunn? Sure as hell he wasn't at the Lazy L. Was he stalking them even now? In the dark, nothing made sense. The saguaros all looked like men. Like men's shadows. Like the shadows of men with guns.

Randy bent down, looked at Langley. The man didn't move.

"Jesus, Slicker, are you dead?"

His voice floated out of his mouth, startled him. It was so damned quiet. He could no longer hear the hoofbeats from Lassiter's horse. An emptiness rose up around him, suffocating, strangling.

Randy glanced around, his eyes wide with fear. Steeling himself, he touched Langley's face, felt his cheek. His flesh was warm. Encouraged, Randy shook the man, grabbing him by the shoulders with his hands.

"Slicker . . . Slicker . . . wake up, man!"

Langley groaned.

Randy drew in a full breath. Langley was alive!

"Hold up," said Jason Coker to Cantwell.

Cantwell pulled on the reins. The horse stopped quickly. The rope on the saddle horn went slack.

Coker and Burns rode back down the rope to Randall.

They looked down at the dark shape.

"Is he still alive?" asked Burns.

"You hold a match, we'll check." Both men dismounted. Jason turned Randall over with a kick. A low moan escaped from Jed's lips. Jason grabbed his collar, wrenched him to a sitting position. A flap of skin hung from Jed's cheek. His face was bruised, bloodied.

Paul Burns struck a match, held it close to Randall's face.

"You going to tell us about Gunn now?" said Coker.

Jed's eyes blinked. His lips were bruised, swollen. He made a sound in his throat.

"Huh? What's that? Tell us where Yire lives. We know Gunn's there. You just give us directions, Randall."

Jed made another sound. Then his eyes went wide as the match burned down in Burns' fingers. The match went out as Burns cursed.

"Go to hell, Coker," croaked Randall.

Coker drew back a fist, hurled it at Randall's face. The smack of fist to flesh resounded in the dull night air. Randall's head snapped back and he fell over.

Burns felt Jed's legs.

"Broke," he said to Coker. "Both of 'em."

"The bastard," Coker hissed. "Come on."

Both men remounted, rode back to Cantwell's horse.

"Did he talk?" asked Cantwell.

"Turn around, Pete," said Coker, "drag the bastard up to the Elk's Head and cut him loose. I don't give a damn if he lives or dies."

Cantwell said nothing. He turned his horse, kicked the animal into a gallop. Behind him, Randall's body bounced and jerked on the rope. Randall made no sound. Coker and Burns rode on ahead, back toward Pima Flat.

T.O. came into town from the north. His side pained him some. The bottle in his saddle bags was empty, though, and he felt only a distant pain. His pants were slick with blood, but he paid no attention to that.

He swung off in front of the hotel, limped inside the lobby.

"Gunn here?" he asked the clerk.

"Room, ah, ten," he said. "You're hurt, Mister Lassiter. Want me to fetch the barber if he'll come?"

"Too late for that," said Lassiter. "You just get me up to that room."

Gunn opened the door, saw the clerk holding on to T.O. He saw the blood, the wild look in Lassiter's eyes.

"Thanks, Nick," said Lassiter, lurching forward under his own power.

"You better talk him into letting the barber take a look at that leg," said Nick.

"No!" said T.O. vehemently. "Go on, Nick, and mind your danged business."

Gunn held T.O. to keep him from falling and then closed the door. He led the rancher to the couch, eased him down gently.

"Leg's gonna stiffen up on me if I set too long," said T.O. "Good to see your face, son. Coker around?"

"Never mind, old-timer. We'll look at that leg." Gunn examined him. T.O. winced at certain touches. The bullet had gone clean through. The blood was starting to stiffen. But he'd lost a pint, at least. Gunn brought the pitcher and a cloth, washed the wound clean as best he could. The barber couldn't do much. Pack it with salve, bandage it. But Lassiter would probably lose the leg. There were bits of bone sticking out the backside and when Lassiter moved they were most likely chewing up his meat. Gangrene would set in and . . .

"Verdict?"

"Bad, T.O. Bullet caught your hip bone and splintered it. Bullet went on through. Now, what in hell brings you out tonight?"

Lassiter told Gunn all that had happened.

Gunn listened in admiration. But T.O. had left Esmerelda alone. If Coker knew that, and he would eventually, she was in danger. Coker would go to any extreme, Gunn knew. He'd done it before, up in Colorado. He'd do it now. It was his move, and he wasn't sure what it should be. Coker was gone. He could account for Randy and another man. But that left three more.

While he was trying to decide what to do, Lassiter passed out.

First things first. Gunn went to the lobby, told Nick to get a buckboard and roust out the barber. Nick wasted no time and in ten minutes, they moved Lassiter onto the buckboard. The barber told Gunn where he lived and drove off with his unconscious patient and twenty dollars of Gunn's money.

Gunn made up his mind.

He couldn't wait in the hotel room for Coker. Not now. He had to find out what happened to Randall and try to get Esmerelda off the ranch. His horse was still standing up the street and he made his way for it.

Esquire snorted and stamped a forefoot.

As he reached for the reins wrapped around the hitch rail, Gunn heard a low sound.

"Mister Gunn," someone whispered.

Gunn's hand flashed to his pistol-butt.

"Don't shoot," said the voice. "It's me, Willa."

Gunn peered into the darkness between two buildings. There was a flash of white and then he saw her face.

"Come here," she said.

Gunn walked toward her, wary. His palm rested on the pistol butt, his fingers wrapped around it, ready to draw.

Coker reined up at the road. Burns hauled in, too.

Behind them, Cantwell had slowed to a walk, his horse refusing to run with the dead weight dragging.

"Listen," said Jason Coker, looking down the road, to the east.

A mile or so away, they could see dust shimmering in the faint moonlight. Then, they heard the hoofbeats.

"Someone's comin' hell-bent-for-leather," said Burns.

"Could be Randy," said Coker.

"Or that Gunn feller."

"We'll see." Coker spurred his horse into a stand of saguaro on the other side of the road. "Lay low," he called to Burns. "Get Cantwell to hold up."

Burns rode back to Cantwell, halted him. Then he rode back, flanked the road opposite Coker.

Randy and Langley rode into view. Their horses were lathered and when Coker rode out into view, both men dragged on the reins. The horses veered, skidded to a stop in a swirling cloud of dust.

"You tryin' to kill your horses?" Coker asked his son.

"Pa, Lassiter headed for town, you see him?"

"No."

"Well, he's sidin' with Gunn, and I think Langley here drew some blood."

"I got him all right. Probably dead by now."

Randy told his father what had happened. Cantwell rode up, checked Randall.

"He alive?" Coker asked.

"Still breathin'," said Pete. He don't look much like a man no more. And he's plumb out cold."

Coker told Langley and Randy that Gunn was holed up at Yire's and Yire had lit a shuck.

"So now what, Pa?"

"Gunn will show up, but we're going to make it certain sure. Randy, you take my horse and Burns there. Go back to Lassiter's and bring that gal of his into town. No hitches. Langley, you trade horses with Cantwell. We'll walk them down so they won't founder. You bring the gal to the Pozo, Randy. Me and the boys will meet you there. We'll keep the place open. Got a good view of the hotel and the Elk's Head. Anyway Gunn comes, we'll be ready for him."

The switch was made. Randy and Burns rode back toward the Lazy L. Langley dragged Jed Randall at a walk, behind Coker and Cantwell.

Coker kept silent, alone with his thoughts.

Too many things were going haywire. Gunn was out of reach and now Lassiter was trying to buy in. Randall was useless now, except as a goad. He'd be dead before morning and no loss there. He couldn't understand why a man would fail to face facts. Randall should have seen that his back was to a wall and gone ahead and gotten out of it. Most men would have done that. But there was something about Gunn that inspired such loyalty. He didn't savvy what it was, but any man who gave up his life for another was a damned fool.

The three riders reached the edge of town.

A buckboard rattled ahead of them, up one of the roads.

Coker pulled up.

"Who's that?" he asked.

"Casey," said Burns.

Langley rode up next to them and stopped.

"The barber," he said. "Lives up there, past that chunk of rocks."

Coker saw a light beyond the rocks, then another and another as his eyes grew accustomed to looking through the dark. Houses were scattered on a hillside above the town. None were close together, but the road wound through them like binding twine.

"What the hell's the barber doing this time of night?"

"Beats me," said Burns.

"Well, find out," said Coker. "Langley, ride on in, get rid of that bastard on the rope. Randall's getting on my nerves."

Langley rode past. Coker looked down. Randall had bounced onto his back. He stared straight ahead, his mouth open, his jaw slack. No sign of life. His face was blackened, misshapen from striking rocks. His pants were rubbed off at the calves and knees. The legs, broken, twisted crazily.

"Hey, Coker," called Burns, who had stopped the wagon. "Better get over here."

Coker rode over. Burns had his pistol out. Casey

had his hands up.

"What's up, Burns?"

"Feller's got Lassiter in the back of the wagon. Sure enough, Slicker called it right. He got tagged with a .44-.40."

Coker looked at the barber, then in the wagon.

Lassiter stirred, half sat-up. Blinked.

"You Coker?" he asked.

"I'm Jason Coker."

"Wanted to see your face before you fry in hell," said Lassiter and lay back down.

"Get him out of there, Burns," ordered Coker, taut with anger.

"Man's in a bad way," said Casey. "I'm takin' him home to make his last moments some peaceful."

"We'll take care of him," said Coker. "You'll be on your way."

Burns lifted Lassiter from the wagon, put him in his saddle. He climbed up behind him. Lassiter sagged in the saddle. The pain was back and it burned through his brain like a blacksmith's furnace.

"Mister," said Casey, looking up at Coker, "what you're doing is mighty inhumane."

"Was I you, Casey," said Coker, "I'd stay out of it. It's not likely Gunn or any of his friends will be alive much longer. You buy in on the wrong side, you might join 'em."

Casey clucked to his horse, slapped the reins and the buckboard moved up the road.

"This feller's bleedin'," said Burns.

Coker touched spurs to his horse.

"Let him bleed, dammit," snarled Coker. "That's what we came here for. Blood!"

CHAPTER FOURTEEN

Willa talked fast, in a high thin whisper that was on the edge of hysteria. "I saw them cross the street, go to the livery," she said. "With Jed in front of them. He had something in his mouth. I waited, came out of the Elk's Head and slipped to the back of the stables. They want him to talk, Gunn, to tell them where they could find you."

"Where's Jed now?" Gunn's voice was cold as gunmetal. His face hardened into a mask.

"They—they dragged him. Out there, east. I heard him bouncing over the ground. It was horrible. I—I wanted to scream, to run out there and cut him loose. But I was scared. Plumb scared."

"Well, Willa, you couldn't have done anything. They'd have cut you down."

"I—I want to help. But I'm still scared. I never saw anything so cruel!"

"I'm on my way to find Jed now. At least you gave me a direction."

"Can I go with you? I—I can ride. I can get a horse from the livery."

Before Gunn could reply, they both turned and

saw the horse coming down the street. Dragging something behind it. Gunn melted into the shadows with Willa. They both peered from the side of the building.

"That—that's Langley. One of the men with Coker." Willa's voice squeaked and Gunn thought she was just about to go over the edge.

"Shhh!" he whispered.

Langley pulled up in front of the hotel, dismounted. He walked back to the end of the drag rope and pulled a knife. The knife flashed as he cut the rope.

"That's Jed!" screamed Willa.

Langley whirled, drew his pistol.

Gunn froze, his eyes locked on the man with the pistol in one hand, knife in the other.

Willa began sobbing. Loudly.

There was nothing Gunn could do about it. Langley went into a crouch, got behind Jed's body. He lifted it up, squatted behind it for protection. Jed's head hung to one side.

"Langley!" called Gunn.

"I'm Langley!"

"Gunn."

"Come out, bastard! Your friend's done bought it."

Laughter.

Gunn's insides churned. He felt the hatred rising in him.

He could not see Langley well, and it was a long shot even if he could. Still, he wanted Langley. Wanted him bad.

The decision was taken away from him in the next

moment. Willa shoved past him and started running toward Langley.

"Don't shoot her!" Gunn warned.

"Jed! Jed!" she screamed, tripping over her skirt, recovering, racing straight for Langley's gun. She was between Gunn and the hardcase, so neither had a clear shot of the other.

"Dammit, Willa," Gunn muttered.

She stumbled, almost fell. As she reached Jed, Langley stood up, grabbed her. Jed's body fell with a sickening thud.

Gunn knew his friend was dead. The body didn't move. No sign of feeling. Just a dark lump out there in the street, a strand of rope tied around its wrists.

Langley put the knife to Willa's throat.

"Back off, Gunn, or I saw through this gal's neck."

As Gunn watched in horror, Langley dragged Willa to his horse, threw her over the saddle. He climbed up, holstering his pistol, but keeping his knife on her. He sat back of the cantle, turned the horse around and rode back in the direction he had come from.

Gunn had a clear shot. He cocked his pistol, took aim.

Langley hunched over then, and the opportunity was gone.

Cursing, Gunn rammed his pistol back in its holster, letting the hammer down, and raced across the street.

Jed lay there, twisted and misshapen. Gunn knelt, lifted up his friend's head.

"Jed?"

Then he saw his face. Black with blood, hammered into a grotesque shape. No resemblance to the young man he had seen only hours before. Gunn looked at his scraped body, his broken legs. He thought of Jed's last moments of life. His last hours. Hell, pure hell.

People came out of the Elk's Head, looked down at Gunn sadly. No one spoke.

Gunn looked at them. "This was my friend. A good cowhand. Will some of you take care of his body while I find the men who did this?"

"Sure," said someone, "we'll take care of him. We knew Randall. He was okay."

"Was that Willa out here?" asked a heavy young woman.

"Yes. The bastard that did this kidnapped her at knifepoint."

Gretchen screamed, fainted.

Some Mexicans in the Pozo, seeing Gunn, went back inside. They wanted no part of his trouble.

Gunn walked back to Esquire, slipped the reins loose and climbed into the saddle.

Sanity returned after a moment.

Langley had brought Jed's body in. All right. But where, then, was Coker and the rest of his men? Where was Randy? He decided not to ride down the main street of town. Langley could be waiting for him somewhere beyond the center. Likely was. Gunn kicked Esquire, rode between the livery and the stage stop, into open country. There was no other street on that side of town.

No houses. Just space, cactus, dark.

He rode east, until the main street ran out and

then he turned toward the road.

His first inkling of trouble was when Esquire's ears perked up and the animal whinnied. And then his own scalp prickled.

Firelight on the road. A campfire, the smell of burning mesquite.

Not on the road. Beyond, near a saguaro.

Esquire slowed to a walk without any urging by Gunn. The horse slowed and whickered, blowing air through nostrils and mouth, ruffling his lips.

Closer now, the horse stepping warily. Firelight flickering insanely. And a man standing there, illuminated by the flames.

Gunn drew the reins back hard.

Something was wrong. There was something familiar about the man. The man didn't move and Gunn saw why.

He was bound.

Tied to the saguaro. His eyes flashed with light and he wore no hat. His face glimmered in the light.

Gunn cursed under his breath.

T.O. Lassiter stared straight at him, across the dark, the space, the eerie empty road.

The hackles rose on the back of Gunn's neck. And something inside him went cold.

"I—I can't stand it here anymore," complained Jenny Lee. "I thought I could wait here for him, but I can't."

Tom Yire stood at the window, looking down at the far-off lights of Pima Flat. Not so far away, but on the slope, with the broken ground in between, the lights looked distant. His palsy had stopped, visibly, but inside he was still shaking.

He smoked a pipe and the smoke curled up from the bowl, smeared the air with ghostly tracks.

Jenny Lee stood behind him, away from the window, as if afraid to look out. It had been this way for the past twenty minutes. He was calming down; she was nervous.

"It would be dangerous for either of us to go back down there. I'm telling you, Jenny, anyone connected with Gunn is in danger. Coker's crazy. His men are crazy."

"I don't care! I love him, Tom! Don't you understand that? I love him."

He turned to her, looked at her with sad eyes.

"It's useless, Jenny. He can't beat them. He'll be dead before morning."

"Damn you!" she raged. "Don't talk like that! Gunn's a man! He'll kill them!"

"Do you really believe that?" Tom sighed. He was burnt out. He had stayed too long in Pima Flat. In a dozen towns just like it. Hoping one of them would turn out good, or safe. None of them had. Most had not. Yet he still hoped he would find one that would grow and prosper without the lawless elements that often preyed on new or small towns. Pima Flat had been a quiet, out of the way place for a long time. Until Coker and his men had come. Many in the town had hoped he would not find the man he was looking for; had hoped he would move on and leave them alone. But this had not happened. It was not Gunn's fault, but he would be involved, would involve them all. And, he could not win. Not against such odds. It was too bad Jenny could not see that.

Love had made her blind.

"Yes, I believe that! He beat Coker before and there were a lot of men against him then. He told me what kind of man Coker is. I can't believe that such a man can beat Gunn."

"It's a matter of guns, Jenny Lee. Or firepower. Those men with Coker are not ordinary, either. They're killers. You can see it in their eyes. The way they walk, the way they wear their guns. No, I'm afraid Gunn doesn't stand a chance against such men."

Jenny closed her eyes as if to shut out Tom's words. But the words got through. They got into her mind, but not into her heart. She had to believe that Gunn would win. She had to!

"What can we do to help him, Tom?" she asked, suddenly calm.

"I'm not a gunfighter, Jenny."

"No, but you believe Gunn is right. We could do something. Anything. I just can't stand by helplessly and wait for bad news."

Tom walked to a table, emptied his pipe into a shallow clay bowl. He left the pipe where it was. His tongue hurt from drawing on it too fast and the aftertaste made him slightly queasy. Or was his fear something he could taste? Jenny was right of course. To stay here, holed up like rats, was to deny existence. He had run, but now the waiting was unbearable. Coker might even come looking for Gunn out here. Or, he might decide that any friend of Gunn's was his enemy. There was no safe place. He drew a deep breath, turned to face the anxious Jenny Lee.

"All right," he said. "We'll go into town. I don't

know what we can do. I'll talk to some men. Casey. See if they'll take guns against Coker. I'll take my rifle, though I haven't shot it in months. I'm no good with a handgun, but I'll strap mine on. It may get me killed."

"Tom," she squealed, "I love you!"

"Jenny," he said drily, "that's your trouble. You love too damned much!"

Gretchen Lovelace listened to the talk in the Elk's Head. She stood at the window, wringing her hands.

The horror had drained her.

Jed Randall's face, his dead eyes. She could see them floating out there still. No longer human, no longer bearing Jed's personality. It was hard to imagine him now. She tried to hear his laugh again, see his warm smile, feel his body against hers. But all she could think of was the shapeless mass out there in the street—and the men who had dragged him to his death.

A commotion in the back of the saloon caused Gretchen to turn from the window. Men rose from their tables, left the bar, to surround someone who had entered through the back way of the Elk's Head. Gretchen hurried over to see who had come in, had caused the crowd to surround him.

Casey Houlihan was talking fast, gesticulating with his arms. He carried a pair of pistols on his hips and one tucked in his belt.

The barber, they were saying, had never carried a gun before.

"Well, I'm packin' 'em now. And if you're smart, the lot of you, you'll do the same," Casey said, in his thick Irish brogue. "I'm tellin' you, none of us is safe with those madmen out there." Casey seldom lapsed into the brogue unless he was excited.

"What happened?" asked a man who had been drinking at the bar.

"What happened? I was carryin' poor Lassiter up to me house when Coker and his bunch threatened to kill me. They grabbed T.O. and took him off. I high-tailed it up the hill and got my guns, then drove the ridgeroad back to warn you. I saw them tie Lassiter to a cactus tree and start a fire. For all I know they may be cookin' him alive at this very minute!"

There were gasps from the crowd.

Gretchen crowded forward. "Did you see Willa?"

"Not a sign of her," said Casey. "And I'll have a bit of the juice to calm me nerves. Lord, those are savages, I tell ye, savages!"

Someone gave Casey a drink of whiskey. He downed it in a single gulp, made his way to the bar.

"What's this about Willa?" he asked, as the crowd thinned so that all could see him.

Gretchen told him what had happened.

"And you all saw it and did nothing?"

His look shamed them.

"Some of you are packin' iron, yet you let a poor helpless colleen be taken by a madman. Oh, the Lord help ye!"

"We couldn't do nothin', Casey," said a man called Macabee. "Langley had a knife to her throat."

"We thought it was that man's fight," said another. "Gunn, or whatever his name is. He was there, across the street. Rode out right after."

Casey glared at them.

"I've me buckboard out back. Those of you what's willin' can pile in with rifles and go with me. There may be a chance't to save poor Lassiter before he's burnt to a crisp. I don't know about this Gunn or whose fight it tis, but if we don't take arms against those divils, we'll all be the sorrier for it."

"I'm with you, Casey," said Macabee. "George? Jake? The rest of you fellers. Let's side with Casey and do something for Lassiter."

A cheer rose up.

Gretchen, overcome by the emotion of the moment, ran to Casey, planted a kiss on his forehead. Casey blushed. Men checked their pistols. Someone got the shotgun from behind the bar.

"I'll keep an eye on the bar," Gretchen yelled. "Good luck!"

Men filed out the back. A few lingered, as they had no weapons, but tailed in behind those who were following Casey to the buckboard.

Gretchen walked out, saw them crowding in the wagon. Casey whacked the reins and the horse struggled to pull the weight. There were six men besides Casey on the wagon. The wagon pulled slowly away and the ones who were not going started for home.

Gretchen was alone.

She went back inside the saloon, began cleaning up. Yet she wished she were going with Casey. She wanted to fight back. To shoot, if necessary. Yes, even though she hated violence, she would shoot. Langley, especially. He was the one who had probably dragged Jed to death.

She carried glasses back of the bar, dropped them

in the wooden tub full of water to soak.

The front door opened. Gretchen looked up.

Tom Yire, followed by Jenny Lee Carter, came through the door.

"Where is everybody?" Tom asked.

"Gone. To fight Coker and his men," said Gretchen proudly.

Jenny ran past Tom, rushed up to the bar, leaned over.

"Where's Gunn, Gretchen? Is he—he . . . ?"

"I don't know. He was out there. Jenny, they've got Willa. And T.O. Casey and the others went to fight Coker."

Jenny sighed. There was a chance now. Gunn was alive. And help was on its way.

CHAPTER FIFTEEN

Gunn dismounted, kept low. He pulled his pistol, cocked it.

He saw no one on the fringes of the firelight. Only T.O., still staring straight ahead.

"T.O.!" he called "T.O.!"

"Gunn? That you Gunn?"

"Yes. Are you alone?"

"No—Gunn, look out! They're . . ."

Gunn threw himself headlong, his pistol cushioned by his palm as he fell. From out of the shadows stepped Jason Coker. He hardly recognized him, but it was Coker.

Lassiter's head turned in Coker's direction. Coker held a pistol in his hand. Cocked. He brought it up to Lassiter's temple. Sparks flew in the air, heat waves shimmered above the fire so that the two figures appeared eerily unreal from Gunn's vantage point.

"Throw down your pistol, Gunn, and come up here," said Coker. "Or I'll blow Lassiter's head off."

Gunn swallowed hard.

Coker had him, if he followed instructions. It would be like committing suicide. Once he walked up there, unarmed, Coker would turn the pistol on him and blow him to kingdom come. That wouldn't guarantee Lassiter's freedom, either. Coker smelled blood. He was going to kill somebody, that was certain.

Gunn considered his chances of dropping Coker first. The range was long, fifty yards. An outside chance, if he held high. But the distance was deceptive. Especially with that fire throwing up waves. From his position it looked as if Lassiter was being burned at the stake, but Gunn knew that this couldn't be. The fire had to be a few feet in front of the rancher. But fifty yards, at least. A far piece for a pistol shot. To the head. And that would be the only way he could bring Coker down fast—before he could squeeze the trigger. And even then, he'd be taking a hell of a chance. His dying reflex could jerk the trigger, put an end to Lassiter's life.

"You untie Lassiter, Coker!' Gunn shouted, shifting his position by squirming to his left. This gave him a better angle on Coker and served to confuse any others up there about his position.

"You heard my terms. Hands up, and come this way, or I'll blow this man's head off!"

Gunn licked dry lips. They were getting nowhere this way.

"Don't do it!' croaked Lassiter. "I'm done for anyway. Run for it, Gunn! Run for . . ."

Lassiter's next words were cut off as Coker slashed the rancher across the mouth with his pistol barrel. Lassiter sagged against the ropes. He cried out as cactus spines needled his back.

Gunn cursed under his breath.

His finger tightened on the trigger. The pull was slight. Another touch and the Colt would go off. A sharp stone cut into his leg above the knee. Irritating. He shifted position. Coker still stood there, the barrel of his pistol scant inches from Lassiter's temple.

No, Gunn thought, it was too risky. But Lassiter was right about one thing. He was done for anyway. One way or the other.

If Coker's bullet didn't do him in, the cancer inside him would, in time. Still, Gunn didn't want to sacrifice T.O. to save his own hide. That was not his way.

"I'm going to count to ten, Gunnison!" shouted Coker. "If you don't surrender in that time, I pull the trigger."

Lassiter moved his head, tried to stand up. Gunn watched him, fascinated. Coker saw the movement, but looked out over the fire a moment later. In Gunn's direction.

Lassiter was shaking his head. *No.* Gunn got the message. Damned old man! Tough as a boot.

"One, two, three . . ." Coker began counting.

Gunn crawled closer, keying on a mesquite bush ten or fifteen yards ahead. Beyond that, a saguaro that might provide some cover. And beyond that, the road, open, dangerous. Nothing between the road and Coker. No brush, no cover. He had picked his spot well.

Willa had to be up there, too. A knife at her throat. Coker had him cold, all right.

". . . five . . . six . . . seven . . ." Coker chanted.

Gunn stopped behind the mesquite bush, steadied his hand. It was now or never.

He took aim as Coker intoned, ". . . eight . . . nine . . ."

There was no "ten."

Coker squeezed the trigger.

Lassiter's head snapped as the bullet plowed through his temple into the brain. A cloud of pind spray danced in the firelight. Lassiter's body jerked as if electrified. His limbs sagged. Gunn fired, so angry he jerked.

But Coker was gone. As soon as he had shot Lassiter, he had dropped like a lead weight, out of sight. Gunn's bullet sizzled off into empty space.

He fired again, low, just to keep Coker honest.

And then, all kinds of hell broke loose! Guns boomed. Orange flashes of flame lit the darkness on either side of the saguaro where the dead body of Lassiter hung like a crucified man. Bullets spanged the gritty earth, stung Gunn's face, his eyes. He rolled, firing blindly. A ripping pain sliced his leg. A slug thunked in front of his face and sand burned into his eyes, blinding him.

Frantically, he rubbed the grit from his eyes, backing away in a wriggling slide to escape the withering gunfire that spattered all around him. He returned fire, but the orange flashes never appeared in the same place twice. Coker and his men were not advancing, but they were holding a ragged skirmish line just out of easy pistol range. They were pouring it in with rifles and pistols. Each time Gunn fired, he moved three or four feet to the side and a foot back. His own flashes, he knew, were a dead giveaway in the dark.

Blinking the tears from his eyes, he was startled to see a strange sight. More orange flashes and booming guns, coming from the west, toward town. He saw them, moving closer, all in a cluster. They were firing blindly, but not in his direction.

The firing from across the road died out. Gunn heard men cursing. Still the cluster of firing guns came on, and almost drowned out the sounds of creaking leather, gruff voices, nickering horses. It took him several seconds to see that men were firing from a wagon and the wagon was pulled by a single horse. Now, beyond the firelight, he saw the rumps of horses, something white.

He heard a woman scream.

Willa! And the scream was cut short.

The retreating band of men fired a few shots at the wagon, but then the hoofbeats speeded up and receded from earshot.

Gunn stood up. He felt something hot streaming down his right leg.

The wagon rumbled up, ground to a halt. Men tumbled from the bed, rushed angrily up to the saguaro where Lassiter hung, his head felled across his chest.

"Goddamn!" exclaimed Macabee. "They done plugged T.O. square in the temple."

Gunn limped to the wagon. He recognized the barber, Casey.

"We come as quick as we could," said Casey, "but likely not quick enough."

"No," said Gunn wearily. "Coker shot Lassiter. They tried to shoot me. They've got that gal, Willa. No tellin' what they'll do next."

"Lord, man! You shot?"

"I might have caught a piece of something. A rock, bullet. Doesn't matter. I'm mighty glad to see you fellers."

The men by the wagon crowded around Gunn. They hurled questions at him that he couldn't answer. No one could answer. Maybe Coker could. Why? Why was Lassiter shot? Why were they after Gunn? What were they going to do with Willa Gleeson? Where had they gone? Gunn waved them off, quieted them. And then he spoke.

"You're asking why all this is happening. And you've got a right to know. You came out here, ready to die like Lassiter there. Well, he died. He was dying anyway, and I guess he wanted to die like a man. But he shouldn't have been mixed up in this. Neither should any of you. Coker's an escaped convict from Colorado. Out to kill me. I put him in prison. For the murder of my wife."

The men listened. They nodded. Gunn told them all of it and he didn't apologize. He said it was his fight but he'd lost two good friends tonight and now he had to go off and think.

"But Coker won't let it lie," he warned them. "He won't give up. He'll kill anybody who gets in his way to get at me. You don't have to buy into this game. I'm much obliged you came to help—whether for Willa or T.O. or me. Coker ruined a town or two in his day. I hope he doesn't ruin yours."

Gunn left them there, went up to the saguaro where Lassiter still hung. He holstered his pistol, drew his knife. It was a knife made in Mexico, given to him by a friend he helped one time. It had an eagle's head on the brass handle that wrapped around the elk's antler. Hand-carved. The blade was engraved. The legend, in Spanish, read: *No me saques sin razon, ni me guardes sin honor.* "Do not draw me without reason, nor keep me without honor."

He had reason now.

He cut the rope that bound Lassiter, grabbed the body before it could fall. He lifted it tenderly. The side of T.O.'s head had been blown away. He weighed no more than a child. He was dead. And Coker had killed him. Mercilessly. Without heart. In cold blood. Jesus, in cold blood!

Gunn carried the body to the wagon, lay it gently down in the bed.

"His daughter will want to talk to you about the burial," Gunn told Casey, "but I'll pay the undertaker's fee."

"Ain't no undertaker. My name's Casey Houlihan, Mister Gunn. I'll see to it that the missus wraps the body in a winding sheet and we'll tack together a pine box for T.O."

"Casey, you're a good man. All of you probably saved my life. I was outgunned and sore short of hiding places when you came up. I won't forget it. And Coker will pay for murdering T.O."

"You get him, Gunn, and we'll call it square," said Casey. The others assented with an assortment of affirmative grunts.

"One more thing," said Gunn. "Can one of you ride out to the Lazy L and tell T.O.'s daughter? I want to get to tracking those men, see if I can bring Willa out of this alive."

"But that wound . . . you need . . ."

Gunn left the others, stalking off across the empty ground to where he had left Esquire. The pain in his leg told him that he still had a chunk of lead or rock in his leg. And, from the fresh bleeding, whatever was in there might be sawing through an artery.

Esmerelda dreamed she was back in Houston. But the dream was all cock-eyed. The town was down under the ground and the stairs that led upward really bent down. She was surrounded by fine ladies dressed in the latest fashion but when she spoke to them, they turned their faces. The backs of their heads were covered with smiling masks, chalky masks fixed with permanent smiles. The men swayed to and fro on saddle-shaped swings and these had no faces at all. The higher she walked, the deeper underground she went until finally she reached a huge cavern where wild horses screamed and kicked. They were packed in there like sardines, with flaring tails and manes, kicking and squealing. She drew back, but they surged toward her and the lead horse had the face of a man . . . her father's face, and then the face dissolved, melted like candle wax until the horse resembled Gunn and another horse reared up, churning the air with spinning forefeet and its face was that of Randy Coker, grinning, wearing a sloppy hat, smoking a cigarette. She tried to run, but the doorway was no longer there and the horses ran over her, their hooves pounding on the earth, reverberating in her brain as she was buffeted and thrown from side to side. The horses thundered over her and she heard her voice being called from far away.

"L.D., wake up, gal! Wake up, hear?"

Esmerelda blinked her eyes. The room was dark. A shadowy face floated in the darkness, without definition, hollows for eyes, a crease of light for a chin, a faint crack of nose.

"Who . . . what?" she stammered.

"It's me, L.D., Randy, come to fetch you to town. Your pa wants to see you real bad."

Esmerelda jerked up straight, sat up, wide awake. The dream was gone, wisps of it tangling in her mind like unintelligible smoke signals hanging in a dark sky.

"Randy? What are you doing here? In my bedroom?"

Randy laughed and she shrank away, pulling the coverlet up over her breasts.

"Why, hell, Esmerelda, I done banged on your door until my fist was raw. Came walking in here like a jack miner in hobnail boots. Made all kinds of noise. But you didn't rouse, so I come in here, shook you awake. You must have really been having some dream. You was moaning and talking strange in your sleep."

"You . . ." she bit off what she had meant to say. Randy had said something about her pa. That was the important thing. Not how she felt about his intrusion into this most private of places. "Pa? What's wrong with Pa? Is he dead?"

"Now, now, L.D., don't get yourself in a fret. Old T.O.'s all right. He's just feelin' poorly is all and he asked me and my friend to fetch you real quick."

He sat on the bed. Next to her. She smelled him close to her, his sweat, his leather, the dust clinging to his clothes.

"But I reckon there's no real hurry, it being so late and all."

Randy reached out for her, grabbed a bare shoulder, twisted her toward him.

"No . . ."

"Aw come on now, Paul's outside. He won't come in. There's just you and me here together."

She pushed at him.

Randy held on. His fingers dug savagely into her shoulders as he brought the other hand up to restrain her.

"Don't you go gettin' feisty on me, L.D. I mean to put the boots to you and there ain't nothin' you can do about it."

"Damn you! I'm not something you can throw down and stick like a pig. Get your hands off me before I scream!"

"Scream your little head off if it'll make you feel better, bitch!"

Randy shoved her hard, and she fell back. He ripped her nightgown from her breasts. The tearing sound filled the room. Then his hands were on her breasts, kneading them cruelly, mashing them, grazing the nipples until they hurt. She tried to fight back, but Randy was strong. He tore at her nightgown, ripping it down the side. He grabbed it, pulled, jerked until it came free. He tossed it into the air and it drifted to the floor like a torn flag of surrender. She kicked at him, but he slapped her face until tears stung her eyes, until her bruised mouth bled. Again and again he slapped her until she was still.

She heard him unbuckling his belt. Heard the slither of his trousers sliding down his legs. The clump of his boots on the floor.

He pried her legs apart and his bulk blanketed her vision.

Numbed, she let it happen. Let Randy slide his hard cock into her and pump like a dog humping a bitch in heat.

She wept and he tried to kiss her.

He slapped her again, but continued pumping.

"Damn you," he muttered. "Show some feelings."

"I don't have any. Not for you. Not this way."

He cursed her and then she felt his seed splashing inside her. He fell on her, breathless, and panted against her heaving breasts.

She felt hatred then. Hatred for Randy and for what he had done to her. And beyond the hatred, a realization.

He climbed from her body, dressed silently. She crawled away from him and sat there on the edge of the bed, in shadows, quiet with deep shock.

"Pa didn't send you," she said quietly. "He'd never send an animal like you to fetch me." And the minute she had spoken the words, she knew they were true.

CHAPTER SIXTEEN

Gunn knew he didn't have any time to waste.

Blood oozed out of the wound in his leg. Faster than before. Thick, pumping with every beat of his heart. He could take the pain. The pain was no more than a throbbing worry somewhere in his flesh. But he felt lightheaded, weak-kneed. Shock was the big danger. He could go down, bleed to death. Like going to sleep. Never know what happened.

Esquire stamped and shied from him.

"It's all right, boy," he soothed. "Steady, Esquire."

Gunn's knees turned to mash. The ground teetered, tilted. He steeled himself, hung on.

But something had to be done. Fast. Standing, swaying to keep his balance, he forced himself to feel the wound, probe, with his finger, for the bullet, or chunk of stone. Gritting his teeth, he touched his side, his leg. Felt for the tenderness.

Finger moving like a sightless worm down from his hipbone. In the dark, with the sky wheeling above him, the stars blurring, he touched his flesh, winced as he got closer to the wound. The pain was not localized. His leg was numbing up as if hammered light and steady for a time until the skin lost all feeling but the wound hid itself beneath, only to send out warning throbs to say where it was. His eyes narrowed as his finger slid closer to the blood-oozing hole. He felt as if he was leaning against nothingness.

Esquire sidled away from him.

He heard the men on the road; heard them move away, towards town. Muffled voices as if strained through a tub of water. Hoofbeats fading. And the fire by the saguaro still burning brightly, flickering up there like a beacon, living on hidden oils in the veins of greasewood, brush, mesquite, dead cactus. The fire swam as Gunn's finger found the hole, became drenched with fresh blood.

There was the hole.

He almost passed out when he touched it. He did not look down at it. He would not have been able to see it anyway. Instead, he pushed inside, felt the edges. It was a clean hole. A bullet. A ball of lead. Not a stone.

He withdrew his finger, staggered under the weight of the pain. He forced himself to feel around to the other side. A great dread enveloped him, tightened against his chest like an iron band. The sky came down on him, the ground rushed up fast. And he found the other hole, leaking blood in a small trickle. Inside, with his finger—clean, the angle downward, away from the artery. No lead inside. Dirt, though, the smears of lead in his flesh, in the sinews. He could get by for a time, but the wound needed tending. Needed cleaning, packing. With herbs, salve, whatever would keep the blue streaks from running up his leg, poisoning his heart, shutting off his breath. Gangrene. Death. Agonizing death.

He had to sit down now. Had to pray he could rise again. But there was something he had to do or he would never mount his horse. The blood was running faster now. He could feel its slick heat down his leg, sogging into his pants where the hole was a tattered mass of sheared threads.

Gunn sank to the earth, drew his knife again. He slit the pants down from the hole. It was easier that way. He held the cloth tight, went clear to the boot top. Made a right angle, cut straight back up. Another angle. Tore a clean narrow strip from his trousers. Sheathed the knife. He felt again around the hole. There was some swelling, but a depression where the ball had gone in. Soft there, mushy, spongy.

He took the cloth strip and wrapped it around his leg, high, above the bullet hole. He pulled it tight, gritted his teeth, and held on. Moments slipped by as he crossed the ends and drew them tight. Blood pounded in his temples. Bump, bump, throb, throb. As if he was squeezing blood up to his brain. Taking it from the wound up his throat clear to the temples.

He held the strip tight until the ooze from the wound slowed, then stopped. Quickly, he tied a slip knot, drew it taut enough so that he could release his grip on it. He scrambled, crawled, looking for a piece of wood strong enough to use to tighten the tourniquet. His hands groped the rocky, sandy ground. Esquire looked down, gimlet-eyed, sidled away, wary.

Gunn's fingers found an elongated stone. That would have to do. For the time being. He rammed it inside the knot, tightened the knot. Then he twisted the stone until he could stand it no more. The cloth, drawn up hard as he could draw it, shut off the circulation. The wound stopped pumping out blood. The pain was in another place.

He stood up, holding onto the stone. The tourniquet would not last long. Long enough, he hoped. What he had to do next would tell the tale. If he lived or died. If he could go on and fight or have to hole up with the fevers until his enemies gave up or discovered him.

Gunn knew the dangers. The wound was not serious. Not yet. It was a hole in his leg. Nothing more than that. But it was a bleeding wound and soft lead had passed through his flesh and left traces. Without attention, his leg could stiffen up; he could bleed to death; gangrene could set in; he could pass out from loss of blood and be eaten alive by scorpions, get snake bit or fight off a black cloud of buzzards soon as the sun was high the next morning.

Men had died from less in such places. He tried to fight off such thoughts. Hell, Esquire could kick him to death out of plain fear and he'd wind up the same. Such things had happened. Nearness to a town made no difference. He'd seen men die six feet from a door in Montana, froze up by brain-numbing cold until their senses left them. Seen men die at waterholes on the desert because the sun had baked their brains to stone and they no longer believed their eyes. He had seen the corpses of men who had blown their brains out less than a mile from a waterhole because they could go on no longer. He saw a man eating sand once, thinking it meat and water. He suffocated.

The danger was in letting a serious problem go on too long. Like bleeding. Like a small wound that could attract flies or wolves. Like forgetting that life was often cruel and no man had any privilege at it. Nature didn't work that way. A man survived or didn't. No difference from any animal. Only trouble was, most white men didn't understand that. Some of them thought that they were above the other animals, the red men, the black. Thought they could not get the same diseases, die the same deaths. A mistake. Life was life and it all came out of the same kettle. Death was death, too. It came hard or it came easy, but it came, just the same.

"Come on, boy, we got to move." Gunn spoke quietly to Esquire, limped over to him. He looped the reins over the saddle horn, but did not mount him. Instead, he hung on to the horn to take weight off his leg and urged the horse towards the fire. Esquire moved as Gunn patted him, used the reins sparingly to keep him on course. Together, they crossed the road, came to the fire.

Gunn ground-tied his horse, limped to the fire, favoring his wounded leg.

He searched for an unburned stick, found one nearby. He sat down before the fire, poked one end of the stick into the flames. When it caught and was burning hotly, he loosened the tourniquet. The next part would take all of his strength and courage. He didn't want to pass out, but he had to cauterize the wound, stop the bleeding. There were two points to cauterize, the entrance and exit holes.

He looked at the wound as he stretched out his leg. Blood oozed from the entrance hole, but not excessively. He grabbed the stick, wide enough to cover the hole, and laid it on his bare flesh. Searing pain shot through his flesh, through sinew, muscle and bone. The sickly sweet stench of burning flesh assailed his nostrils. His skin sizzled like bacon as the flaming faggot burned up the wet blood, fried the skin.

Gunn gritted his teeth, moaned with pain.

He pulled the burning stick away, plunged it back into the fire. The wound closed up, the torn blood vessels sealed off. When the stick caught fire again, he lifted his leg slightly, grabbed the flaming faggot and slapped it on the exit wound. The pain almost caused him to pass out. But he held the burning stick there until he could no longer stand it.

He rewrapped his leg, tied the makeshift bandage

tightly, but did not apply a tourniquet. Instead, he put the bandage directly over his wounds, hoping the ride would not cause any further bleeding. He stood up, tested his leg and found it would hold if he did not put all of his weight on it. Later, he could pack the wound, put a fresh bandage on it. He would be sore for a while, but the bullet had evidently been partially spent before striking him. Otherwise he might have had a much worse time of it. A flattening lead ball, especially if it smacked into bone, could do terrible damage to man or animal. The slug that hit Gunn had missed the artery, missed the bone. Perhaps it had struck the ground first and ricochetted into him. The soft lead may have picked up a sliver of rock, too, or sheared off partially as it passed through his leg.

Gunn untied Esquire, climbed up in the saddle.

He had some hard tracking to do and wasn't sure if he could do much while it was still dark. Instead, he hoped to ride in a wide circle around Pima Flat and see if he picked up any sign: a bit of cloth from Willa's dress, a sound, anything at all that would show him where the outlaws had gone.

An hour later, Gunn's leg started to throb. A bad sign. Gangrene could be setting in. Or it could just be that the cauterized tissue was beginning to fill with blood as the veins sought to find new courses in the flesh. He had found no trace of Coker and his men. It was as if the earth had swallowed them up.

Weary, in pain, Gunn rode on for another hour, completing his circle of the empty land surrounding Pima Flat. At the end of his loop, Gunn rode the main road back into town.

The main street was quiet, empty.

The Elk's Head was still open, but El Pozo Seco was dark, the door closed. Gunn put Esquire up in the livery stable, grained him, saw that he had water in his stall.

The hotel had a different clerk.

"Any sign of Coker?" Gunn asked.

"Nope. We got men on watch, didn't you see them?"

Gunn shook his head.

"You Mister Gunn?"

"Yeah."

"Woman in your room. Miss Lovelace."

Gunn took the key, limped upstairs. The pain now was shattering. Blood pounded in his temples. All he wanted was to sleep, try to pick up sign of Coker early in the morning. Who in hell was Miss Lovelace? One of Jed's friends?

Gretchen opened the door for Gunn.

"I heard you coming," she whispered. "I'm Gretchen. They said you were hurt."

She closed the door, locked it.

"What do you want?" Gunn asked, limping to the bed.

"I—I'm a friend of Willa's and Jenny's. I'm worried. Jenny was supposed to meet me here. I brought bandages and medicants to tend to your wound."

Gunn could smell it. The bureau top was crowded with bandages, liniment, ointments, salves. It stank.

"Jenny's here? In town?"

"Yes. She and Tom Yire came back over two hours ago. Tom closed the bar and Jenny went over to the Pozo to get some whiskey. She thought you might need it. That was over an hour ago."

Gunn frowned.

"The cantina's closed," he said.

"I know. I went over there and pounded on the door. Julio didn't answer. They don't usually close this early. I guess after the killings . . ."

"Yeah." Gunn lay down on the bed, groggy with pain. A wave of weariness washed over him. He didn't know how long he could keep his eyes open. He closed them and basked in the darkness. His leg throbbed. He thought about loosening the bandage but the strength seemed to have gone out of him. He couldn't make his hand move. He wanted to take off his boots and just sink into sleep.

Gretchen looked at the tall man for a long time. She was half afraid of him. He was so big, and if cleaned up, rather handsome. His hat brim shadowed his forehead, but he had a strong chin, sensual lips. She could see why Jenny would be attracted to him. Any woman would.

As she stared, Gunn rolled over. His leg was blackened by soot around the dirty bandage. This would never do. She couldn't wait for Jenny any longer. Her man needed attention. She had tended hurt men before. Her mother had been a nurse in the War and had taught her a great deal. To her regret, she had not followed the profession, but had taken what had seemed an easier path. Now, she thought, maybe she could make up for some of that neglect of her own skills.

She took Gunn's hat from under his head. It was crumpled and she straightened it. She hung it from the bureau mirror, then carried pitcher and bowl to the night table next to the bed. She brought fresh bandages, a medicating salve and some iodine, laid it out neatly next to the bowl and pitcher.

In her wrapper pocket she had scissors and straight razor. She took those out, then cut away the makeshift bandage. Gunn didn't stir. She poured water in the bowl, soaked a cloth in it. She swabbed both wounds, wincing when she saw what Gunn had done to himself. Blood oozed from the cauterized wounds, but that was a good sign. The tissue appeared healthy. It was red, not blue. There were no telltale streaks going up or down his leg.

Gretchen had to get Gunn's trousers off. She rolled him over on his back, loosened his beltbuckle, gunbelt. She stripped them off so that she had a better view of his wounds. His shorts came off, as well, and she found herself fascinated with his manly equipment.

She brought swabs over from the bureau, soaked them in iodine. Carefully, gently, she cleaned the wounds. Then she poured iodine in them. Gunn groaned, twitched.

"Sorry," she whispered. "I know it hurts. But you'll be just fine."

Gunn remained asleep. His groans subsided.

She packed the wounds with a healing salve after scrubbing all the soot off his leg. Next, she put gauze over each hole and wrapped the leg with a tight clean bandage. She trimmed it, cut it expertly, tied it tightly.

She took off Gunn's shirt, pulled the covers back on one side of the bed. She eased him over, pulled the covers up over him. He moaned once, but his eyes did not open.

It was quiet in the room.

Jenny was gone. Disappeared. It was not likely she would show up this late. Gretchen looked at Gunn, made up her mind. She could sit in a chair, watch over him, but that was silly. She could keep him warm, sleep in the bed with him. If he got angry, she would leave. She felt a stir in her loins. A thrilling heat that had not been there before.

Quickly, her heart in her throat, she undressed. Her ample figure flowed with light as she bent over, nude, to turn down the wick, blow out the lamp. She climbed into bed, under the covers. She lay there, her heart pounding, for a long time. Her breathing seemed very loud to her.

Would he mind? If she just touched him? He was so close and he smelled so manly. She snuggled close to him, threw an arm across his chest, let it lie there gently.

She kissed his cheek, felt her loins flood with desire.

She took her arm from his chest, found his manhood between his legs. She began kneading the soft flesh, stroking his penis with eager fingers. She began to squirm with need as Gunn's flesh responded. She enclosed his cock with her hand, rubbed it up and down. She felt the blood pulsing in his organ. A thrilling current ran through her veins as Gunn became hard. She stroked his scrotum, touching the wrinkled skin, the straggly hairs. Her hand tingled.

Unable to restrain herself as his penis grew hard and stretched out to full length, she stuck her head under the covers and slid towards him. She kissed his belly, slid down to his pubic mass. She held the cock up, leaned over, slid the crown into her mouth.

A drenching relief warmed her as she drew his member inside her steaming mouth. She suckled him slowly, savoring the lemony tartness of his seeping fluids, drew him deep, her lips encircling the throbbing organ.

Gunn stirred.

She suckled him faster, unwilling to release him. She felt his fingers thread through her hair, knead her scalp. She hunkered up on her knees, got a better grip on him. The covers fell from her shoulders. His cock stood straight up, slightly bowed, and she took the crown deep into her throat. Her lips grazed the root of his swollen stalk and she held him there, swallowing.

"Gretchen? You do it nice. When you get tired of that, I'll give you the rest of it. Any way you want."

"But your leg . . ." she gasped, spewing him out.

"I've got three legs," he laughed, "and two of 'em are in good shape."

Gretchen laughed too, and slid up to him. He took her in his arms and she knew it would be all right.

"You're some man," she sighed. "Some kind of man . . ."

CHAPTER SEVENTEEN

Randy Coker reined his horse up in the darkness. Paul Burns came up behind him. South of town, their path would bring them up behind El Pozo Seco.

Esmerelda tried to jump out of the saddle. Randy's arm squeezed her until she gasped with pain.

"What you stoppin' here for, Randy?" asked Burns.

"Time to gag this little bitch and go the rest of the way on foot. We sure as hell don't want to wake anybody up."

"Yair," said Burns. "You gonna let me take my turn with that wench before we turn her over to your pa."

"You shut up, Burns," said Randy. "I staked this claim."

"Watch your sadd, sonny. You act like a man, but you ain't your daddy yet."

"What's that supposed to mean?"

"Means you act uppity for a damned pup. Your pa's pullin' your weight, sonny. If he goes down, you go with him."

"I can fire your ass."

"Put the money in my hand, asshole. Your bluff is called."

Randy snorted, turned away from Burns. His face blushed red from shame and he toyed with the idea of drawing down on Burns.

"Just try it, sonny."

"Let's get to the Pozo, Burns. We'll settle this later."

Randy stepped down from the saddle, jerked Esmerelda's arm so that she tumbled straight toward the ground. Randy caught her, laughed cruelly. She struggled again, but he slapped her. He pulled a strip of cloth from his pocket, gagged her.

"You walk where I take you," he told her, "or I'll rape you in the ass, next time." He said this in a low voice so Burns could not hear. Esmerelda stared at him in silent rage. He smiled scornfully and pushed her ahead of him as he led his horse toward the cantina.

Jenny Lee struggled with the thongs that bound her hands behind her back.

They were tight, and the leather had been wetted down so that the strands cut into her wrists.

Julio sat there a few feet away, staring up at the ceiling. Sightless.

His throat had been cut.

He was the owner of El Pozo Seco. Or had been. Now he was dead. Stiffening against the front of the bar like a statue. His face turning into weathered leather. His eyes glazing into marbles. His mouth open in surprise and a smile cut below his chin, from ear to ear. Grotesque. The flesh parted like a gutted pit's belly. Hardening like the rest of him into *rigor mortis.*

Jason Coker sat at a table in the center of the room, alone. Fondling an unlit cigar. He did not look at Jenny, but she looked at him.

Wondered what kind of man he was.

Cantwell had done the throat-slitting. And now he sat with Willa, his hands squeezing her breasts every few seconds as if willing her to respond. But Willa had turned into a whimpering child after what had happened. Her eyes darted everywhere and she cringed at the shadows thrown by the coal oil lamps.

Jenny felt sorry for her. Willa had seen Julio die, too.

They all had, and it now seemed so unreal, so impossible that Jenny doubted her own sanity.

Langley emptied the cash box, rummaged behind the bar until he found what he was looking for: a sack full of coins that had been hidden.

"Two double eagles, a bunch of silver," he said. "These Mexes are always hiding money."

Jenny heard the jingle as Langley lifted the sack, grinned inanely at Coker.

"Hid it in a coffee tin."

"Shut up, Langley," said Coker. "I hear something."

They were all quiet, then, listening.

Three taps on the door. The back door. Cantwell pushed Willa aside, drew his pistol. Langley stiffened.

"That's Randy," said Coker. "Let him in, Cantwell."

Cantwell opened the back door.

Randy shoved Esmerelda into the hallway, followed her in. Behind him, Paul Burns locked the door.

"Anybody see you?" asked Jason.

Randy shook his head. He blinked as he saw Willa and Jenny. Esmerelda made muffled sounds through her gag. He took it out.

"Are you Randy's father?" she asked, glaring at Jason. "Well, this animal raped me. I hope Gunn kills you both!"

Jenny rose to her feet, went to Esmerelda.

"Why don't you untie us and let us go, Mister Coker? You won't get Gunn this way."

"You shut up or I'll gag all of you," said Jason. "Randy, get the gals behind the bar."

"Gunn know you're in here?" Randy asked.

"I don't think so. But he will."

"When?"

"Soon. I want to go over my plan first. We don't want to make any mistakes this time."

Randy herded the women behind the bar. Langley pocketed the silver and gold coins, left the empty sack on the floor. Jenny, Willa and Esmerelda sat down. Randy took a stand at one end, Langley on the other.

"No talking," said Randy. "Or we gag you."

Coker, satisfied at his son's tone of authority, began speaking, drawing imaginary lines in the air with his unlit cigar. His cane leaned against the table. The doorway had been sealed off with rags so that the lanterns did not shine through. The window, too, leaked no light. He kept his voice low so that the walls helped muffled the sound. It was important, just then, that no one know they were inside the Pozo.

"Gunn probably tried to track us," he said. "He's one of the best trackers in the country. I doubt if he could read sign in the dark though, and so he'll probably give it up, if he hasn't already. I want all of you to know what we're up against, what we have to do to cover ourselves if he does outguess us.

"My hunch is that he's back at the hotel, getting some shuteye. In the morning he'll backtrack, find our trail. That'll lead him right to the back door."

"He comes in," said Langley, "we'll get him."

"Oh, he'll come in, but not from the back. We don't want him to work for it. We're going to make it easy on him."

"What're you getting at, Pa?"

"All right. He knows we've got that Gleeson gal. He'll do anything to protect a woman. That's one ace we've got. But we've got two more now. The Carter gal was supposed to meet him. She's been with him out at Yire's place. So, he'll want her back. And now we've got Lassiter's kid. I'd say that gives us three aces. Best way to play them is to use them one at a time. Now, he may know about Jenny Lee, or suspect that we've got her. But he doesn't know for sure. And we don't tell him."

Coker paused, thinking it out. He wanted to get up, but his leg was stiffening up on him. They all needed sleep and one of them would have to stand watch. But he had to put these thoughts down while they were still fresh, make the men understand how they could get Gunn and not lose a single man.

"At daybreak, Langley's going to show Gunn the first ace: the one they call Willa."

"Hey, I'm not walking out there with no woman

in front of me. The town's all riled up." Langley fixed Coker with a baleful eye.

"No, it won't work that way," said Jason. "But we want Gunn to come in here. Now we know there are men out there. There'll be one or two we can see come morning. You show them the Gleeson gal at the front door. Tell them to bring Gunn and he can have her. Don't worry, we'll cover you. They'll see rifle barrels poking out at them."

"Then what?" asked Randy, impatient to hear it all.

"Gunn comes over. Langley backs up, the gal in front of him. I wait back there in the dark hallway with a Greener. The minute he walks in, we all cut loose. Cantwell, you'll be in that corner by the door. You can get him from the side. Turn a table over and hide behind it so you don't get your ass shot off."

"It ought to work good," said Cantwell, glad to hear his part of it.

"What about me? Where'll I be?" Randy again, petulant.

"Back of the bar with the other two gals. They'll be standing up, too, so they'll get Gunn's attention. You have a gun on them. He'll know if he makes one move, you'll kill 'em."

"Will I kill them, Pa?"

"Damned right! If he tries anything funny, you shoot either one or both."

"Jesus," said Langley. "You got him wired down tight."

"I think so," said Coker, satisfied. "But, if something should go wrong. And with Gunn it damned sure can, then Burns will be at his back. The minute we see him come out of the hotel, Burns, you'll go out back, circle and come up from the outside."

"Fair enough, I reckon," said Burns. "But I'll be out in the street. With guns at my back."

"You keep your hat on tight, brim turned down and just act like you belonged. You can pull it off if you do it right. No one'll expect it. They'll think we're all in here. It's perfect."

"Maybe so," said Burns. "We'll try 'er."

"Good! Now, get some shuteye. I'll take the first watch. We'll do hour watches. Someone wake me up before dawn. We'll open the doors, so's he can come through the batwings. Cantwell, second watch, Burns, third, Randy, last. Langley, you sleep on through. You got the hard part."

Randy blew out the lamp behind the bar, lay on the floor.

"You gals behave," he said, "or you won't last 'til morning."

Jason blew out the other lamp. The room was dark. He sat at the table, listening first to the breathing, then the snoring. He was not sleepy, but strangely elated. At last, he thought, he had Gunn where he wanted him. In a few hours it would be all over.

Gunn slept fitfully, Gretchen next to him, her plump body nakedly at repose.

Where was Jenny Lee? Was Willa still alive? Where was Coker?

Maybe Jenny had gone back to Yire's to wait for him. No, she would have said something. Coker had her. And he was probably holed up across the street. He couldn't go busting in there, though. That would spell death for Jenny if he had her. No, it was

Coker's move now. If word didn't come before morning, he would track him, make certain. First check the Pozo, front and back. There would be sign.

Finally, he slept.

Someone was shaking him. Groggily, he blinked. Gretchen's face loomed over his. She was whispering. He sat up, rubbed his eyes. The room was hazy with faint light. It was not yet dawn, but that brief time of morning when the sky started to pale and the stars disappeared.

"Gunn, there's a body outside the door. Tapping at it. Wake up."

"I'm awake." He heard it then, a rapping that got louder.

He got out of bed, found his pistol, shook it out of the holster.

"Who's there?" he called.

"Tom. Gunn, open up. It's important."

"A minute, Tom."

Gunn motioned to Gretchen, who sat in bed holding a sheet up over her ample breasts. Then he dressed quickly as she struggled into her clothes. When she was ready, Gunn opened the door.

Tom's face was drawn, his eyes droopy with sleeplessness. He closed the door, leaned against it.

"All right, Tom," Gunn said, smoothing back his hair, looking for his hat. Spotting it on the bureau, he tamped it back in shape. "Let's have it. You find Jenny Lee?"

"No. But I have a good idea where she is. We got trouble. You got trouble."

"Coker?"

"Yeah, Coker. But the message comes from Langley. He's across the street at the Pozo. I think the whole bunch of 'em might be, although we didn't find any horses out back. Back door's locked. Langley came through the batwings holding on to Willa. Had a knife at her throat. Said to tell you to come over, alone, unarmed. Or he'll . . ."

"I know what he'll do."

Gretchen gasped.

"What are you going to do?" she asked.

Gunn slid his hat on, checked his gunbelt.

"It's going to take some thought. Anybody down there to back me?"

"Langley cleared 'em all out. We have a few men who can cover you as long as you don't go inside the Pozo."

"But I'll have to go in."

"Yes. If Willa's to live."

Gunn thought fast. His leg was all right. Sore, but not bleeding. The bandage held tight. He'd have to go in there, but not on Coker's terms. Either way it was a risk. For him, for Willa Gleeson. The trick was to balance the odds back in his favor. Do something Coker didn't expect. Coker was slick. He had men to back him up. He probably had them set up strategically inside the cantina. A couple of men bracing the door, another behind the bar. A couple in the back. Or behind tables. Yes, it would be all set up. Once he walked in there, they'd cut him down. Willa would probably be killed anyway. And maybe he had Jenny Lee.

"Can you stall Langley?"

"I don't think so. Gunn, none of us is used to this. Someone went to get Casey, because he's the only one who's showed much gumption since last night. But if you take Casey with you they'll probably shoot him too. The men think that it's a matter of an exchange. You for Willa."

"Jesus," said Gunn. "You think Coker goes by any rules? He'll likely kill a half dozen before he leaves, even if I do go in there."

Tom was uncomfortable, he knew. He shifted his weight, looked down at the floor sheepishly. What galled him was that the town believed Coker. Or Langley. Believed that he'd just kill Gunn and let Willa go. Likely as not he'd kill a few just to keep their mouths shut. Threaten them. That was Coker's way. No one was safe as long as he was alive, inside the town. No, this wasn't going to be a simple exchange. It would serve no purpose. Not in the long run.

Gretchen sidled up to Gunn, her face blanched with fear.

"Poor Willa," she said. "You've got to get her away from those men. Isn't there some way you can do it without getting killed?"

"I don't know," Gunn said. "I doubt it. No, there'll be innocent blood spilled. Coker holds the deck. It's his game. But there might be a way to stop him. Or get him off balance. Tom, you know of any Mexicans here who have burros?"

"Burros? Hell, I don't see . . ."

"Just answer me."

"Well, yeah, there's burros. Mexicans put a lot of stock in them."

"Can I buy a couple? Three?"

Tom stood away from the door, scratched his head under his hat.

"Maybe. You might buy some . . . but you'd pay dear."

"All right. Tell Langley you're trying to find me. Meet me out back and take me to where I can get those burros."

"He won't believe me."

"Nothing he can do, can he? He won't come over here and if I'm not there he has to sweat it out."

"I—I guess you're right."

"Gretchen, you get me some bottles full of coal oil. Fill 'em full, put a long strip of cloth in each one. Set 'em out back. Come on, Tom, we're wasting time."

Gretchen stood there, her mouth open. Gunn kissed her on the cheek, hurried Tom out the door. There was a lot to do and no time to do it. If his plan worked, he'd have a chance to get Coker off balance, maybe even put him down. But he needed those burros. Poor dumb animals. If a man wouldn't help him, then maybe the burros would.

Gunn smiled. It was ironic, in a way.

Use an ass to catch an ass. Coker wouldn't appreciate it, but the man had no sense of humor.

CHAPTER EIGHTEEN

The Mexican was suspicious of the two men who walked up to his *jacal.* His name was Pepe Cornejo and he owned five burros.

He also had a garden, a wife and two small daughters. His hand dug well helped him irrigate his small garden, but the work was hard. He had chickens, too, and two mangy skeletal dogs that slunk behind the thatched shack when Gunn and Tom walked up to the *jacal.*

Tom made the introductions in English.

"What is it you want, *senores?"* asked Pepe. "Why do you come so early in the morning to see a poor *peon?*

"Quiero a comprar tres burros," said Gunn.

"But I do not have any burros to sell," said Pepe in Spanish.

"I need them only for a little while. I will pay you for them, but when I am finished, I will give them back to you. You may keep the money."

Pepe backed away from the strange *gringo* with his strange offer. "I need my burros," he said. "They are not used to hard work. They are like pets to us."

"They are just going to be my companions for a little while," said Gunn.

"You are the *gringo* who killed those men in the Pozo yesterday."

"I am," said Gunn.

"And what will you do with the burros?"

"It is a plan I have. I have to fight some more men. By myself. I thought I would use the burros for concealment and to confuse them."

"Three burros could not confuse anyone, *Senor.*"

"No, you are probably right, Pepe. It would be better if I could drive a herd of cattle through the Poza and run with them. But I have no cattle."

"And no burros."

"No. No burros."

"I must consider this. Burros are very dear. Very dear."

"I know. But a horse is too big and horses are too common. The burros would do me just fine. For a little while. *Un poco tiempo.*"

Pepe shook his head, walked over to the *jacal* and talked quietly with his wife. It seemed to Gunn that they talked a long time, but it was actually less than two minutes. Finally, the peon came out again and spoke to Gunn.

"How much would you pay for each burro?" he asked.

"I will pay twenty dollars in gold for each burro."

"That is a lot of money. More than we see in a year."

"It is too little, but it is fair."

"I would have to ride to Tucson to buy other burros. I may have to ride even farther than that. I might have to ride all the way to California, or down into Mexico to find such fine burros as these."

"You may get these back. If the bad *gringos* do not shoot them."

"Ah, that is another consideration. The killing of a pet is a serious thing."

"That is why I am going to pay you forty dollars more in gold for the three little burros, Pepe. That will be one hundred gold dollars in your pocket. You can buy more burros and you can buy pretty dresses for your daughters and you can buy presents for your lovely and most gracious wife. With this hundred dollars you can do much for your family and you may still get your burros back. I do not think the men I am after care much to kill burros. They would not wish to waste good bullets on such humble animals."

Pepe laughed, slapped his leg. He grinned at Gunn with the few good teeth he had left.

"They would rather you took their lead, eh, *Senor*. Well, I will sell you three burros, but I must have the gold in my hand."

Gunn sat down, tugged at a boot heel. Pepe watched in fascination. Tom as well. The heel twisted on a screwed plate. In the hollow of the heel were five gold pieces. Double Eagles.

"That is a very strange place to carry money," said Pepe.

"It is one of several. I am often alone, far from banks and sometimes gold is the only exchange."

"You are a smart man."

Pepe took the gold pieces and led Gunn to the pen where the burros were standing in a bunch. They were small, mouse-colored, with no marks of the pack on their hides. Gunn selected two jacks and a jenny. He led them out of the pen with the short rope halters Pepe provided. He waved to the Mexican family and pulled and burros behind him.

"You can go tell Langley I'll be there in fifteen minutes, Tom," said Gunn. "Tell him you found me sleeping with a Mexican woman. Now, run, so you'll be out of breath when you get there!"

Tom looked at Gunn as though the latter had lost his senses.

"I still don't . . ."

"Just get everyone out of my way. No one on the street. No mention of these burros. If this is going to work it's got to be a complete surprise. Now, run, Tom, run!"

Tom took off at a lope. Gunn spoke soothingly to the burros, got them into a run. He made a game of it and the burros chased him to the back of the hotel. There, Gretchen was waiting. She had three bottles of coal oil filled, each with a cloth wick. She was filling a fourth.

"That's enough," he said. "Thanks. Now stay out of sight, Gretchen."

"Gunn, I'll pray for you. And Willa too. And Jenny Lee."

"You do that." he said.

He stuck a bottle in each back pocket, another in his belt after loosening it. At the edge of the building he half-opened a small box of sulphur matches, stuck them in an upper vest pocket where they'd be handy. Then, he drew his pistol, took out the roll of bills in the empty chamber. He put a bullet in the empty chamber. There would be no quarter given on this one. He shoved the pistol behind him, down inside his belt near the small of his back. He drew a deep breath and grabbed the bottle from his waistband. This he held in his left hand. He moved the burros out ahead of him, ducked in among them. This would be the hard part. He crowded them ahead of him down the lane between the hotel and the next building. His course would take him to the street. He had but to cross it unseen and go through the batwing doors of the Pozo. That was all he had to do.

And it was everything.

Langley listened to what Yire had to say.

"I don't believe you," he said.

"Well, it's the truth. Gunn's coming."

"Alone?"

"Yes," Tom lied. "Alone."

Willa stood there, frail and frightened, Langley's arm around her waist, a knife blade at her throat. Her eyes were wide with fear. Tom backed away, told the men he saw to get inside.

"This is Gunn's party," he told them. "Everybody out of sight until it's all over."

The street was empty.

Langley backed into the saloon. The batwing doors swung. The hinges creaked.

"Well?" asked Coker, from the back hallway.

"He's a-coming," said Langley.

"Make sure," said Coker. "Keep the gal in front of you. Burns, you get moving. Go out front."

Coker's eyes gleamed. He was ready. The room seemed to breathe of its own accord. The sun was coming up now and light streamed through the windows on a slant. Motes of dust danced in the doorway like fairy lights. Langley moved close to the batwings. He could see over them. Burns slipped out the back door, started to circle the building.

It was quiet for a long while.

"See anything?" Cantwell asked.

"Shh!" warned Coker.

Langley's eyes darted everywhere. He heard something. He tensed. Quickly, he slid the knife back in its sheath, drew his pistol.

"I see something," he said.

"What?" asked Coker in a loud whisper. "Gunn? Is it Gunn?"

"Jesus, I don't know. Comin' from over across the street. Be damned. It's a pack of burros."

Gunn hunched low. Midway across the street, the burros started to balk. The lead one, the jenny, wanted to turn up the street. Gunn hit one of the jacks with his shoulder, bumping him into the jenny. At the same time, he jerked hard on the halter ropes, pulling them toward the Pozo. The jenny changed direction. The burros, skittery now, started to trot. Gunn had to run to keep up. But they were going the right way. He could not see ahead of him, but he knew where the Pozo was. He had to get them to go right through the door and that would be the hardest part of all.

The jenny changed direction. The burros, skittery now, started to trot. Gunn had to run to keep up. But they were going the right way. He could not see ahead of him, but he knew where the Pozo was. He had to get them to go right through the door and that would be the hardest part of all.

"Hey!" yelled Langley, then. "Get them fuckin' burros outta there!"

The burros balked, and Gunn muscled them forward. Toward Langley's voice. Now, between their shoulders, he could see the front of the cantina. The window on the left, part of the doorway.

"Whoo, burros!" yelled Langley, trying to shoo them away.

Gunn managed a smile. Langley hadn't spotted him yet. There was still a chance he could make it.

But he wasn't there yet.

"What the hell's going on there, Langley?" asked Coker, angered.

"A bunch of burros, three or four of them, coming straight for the door," said Langley. "Beats all . . ."

"You dumb bastard. Count their fucking legs."

"Huh?"

"That's Gunn's doin', dammit. He's up to something. Look around. He's trying to get your attention."

Langley stretched his neck, stood on tiptoes. The burros were out of sight now, hidden by the batwing doors. He couldn't see them, even by stretching.

Maybe they'd turned.

No, he heard them. They were coming fast now. Honking and bleating all of a sudden. As if someone was prodding them.

Someone!

Langley forgot about Willa, then. He shoved her

aside, rushed to the door. His first mistake.

Coker saw him do this and half rose from his chair behind the overturned table in the back hallway. This was just what he didn't want to happen. Any deviation from the plan could spell disaster.

"Langley! Langley, get back. Get the girl!"

Willa staggered, regained her footing. She looked up, saw Jenny Lee and Esmerelda looking at her, staring at her with frantic eyes. Beside them, Randy Coker stood, a puzzled look on his face. He held a gun up to Jenny's head.

"Stay down, girl," warned Cantwell. "You get in the way, you're liable to die right quick."

"Run!" yelled Esmerelda.

Randy's blood froze. Savagely, he turned on her, slashed her with the barrel of his pistol. She ducked, and the barrel flashed by her face harmlessly. Jenny, seeing her advantage, shoved Randy. He fell, tumbling over Esmerelda. His pistol fired, the bullet plowing through the hard-packed dirt back of the bar.

Langley started to turn when he heard the shot.

At the same moment, the burros charged the door. He saw them coming and raised his pistol to fire.

Too late.

Three burros, kicking their heels, charging, bleating, rammed their way through the batwings, knocking him down. The jenny's head butted him square in the groin.

Langley screamed in pain, went down. Hooves smashed into his gut, his shoulders, his legs.

Gunn released his grip on the halter ropes, backed

away from the burros. He kicked the lagging jack in the rump, snatched the matches from his pocket. He pulled one free, struck it, lit the oil-soaked rag in the bottle of coal oil he held in his left hand. As the burros raced, kicking and honking through the batwings, he tossed the bottle through the window on his left. He hurled it with force, hoping the flame wouldn't go out.

The glass shattered.

A streak of fire spread along the dirt floor.

Quickly, Gunn raced to the space between the window and the batwing doors. He heard Langley go down, screaming. He took a bottle from his back pocket, struck another match. Lit it, threw it inside. Then, the other bottle, while the match still flared. He held on to this one until it was burning well. Then he stepped up to the doors, drew back and hurled it as hard as he could over the top of the doors.

Men shouted. Guns boomed.

Splinters flew from the batwings.

Seconds later, Willa came crashing through the doors. Gunn grabbed her, hurled her down, out of danger. Bullets whizzed through the window he had broken. He heard the crackle of flames. Women's voices screaming.

The bar caught fire. One of the tables was aflame.

Cantwell's clothes caught when he tried to get out of the corner.

Coker swore, held the cocked Greener, unwilling to believe that Gunn had done all this without once showing his face.

Where in hell was Randy?

Randy was down, straddled by Jenny and Esmerelda.

He groped for his pistol.

Smoke filled the air. The smell of burning oil.

Cantwell was screaming, rolling on the floor.

The burros raced around the room, panicked by the smell of smoke, the crackle of flames. They kicked and squealed, tried to find an escape route.

Langley got up, groped his way through the smoke, rubbing his eyes. He had lost his pistol. A burro grazed him and he kicked at it angrily. Coker watched the scene in utter disgust. He could see what was happening. Willa had escaped. Gunn was outside. Randy was behind the bar and out of action, for some reason. Cantwell was trying to get the flames out. The back of his shirt was on fire.

It was mass confusion.

And still, Gunn had not come through the door!

Gunn knew he was going to have to go in. He had distinctly heard Jenny's voice. And another woman's.

Whose?

There was no gunfire inside. Were they all still waiting for him. He heard grunts and groans, curses and the hooting of the burros, the crash of chairs and tables.

If he went in low, rolled to his left, he might make it. He would have the bar for protection if he scrambled for it. Unless someone was there. No doubt Coker had planned for this possibility. But some of the men inside were out of commission. Temporarily, at least.

He had to make a decision fast.

Maybe Coker had already killed Jenny. And the other woman. He no longer heard their screams.

Then, out of the corner of his eye, he saw movement. Turning, he saw a man step from between the buildings. The man had a pistol and he was less than ten yards away.

Gunn, emptyhanded, watched as the man raised his pistol to fire. He heard the lonesome sound of the hammer being cocked.

Langley found his pistol, picked it up.

Cantwell got the flames out on his shirt back, staggered to his feet.

"Langley, check the bar!" Coker yelled. "Cantwell, watch the door!"

Coker watched as Cantwell reloaded. He had been the only one shooting and he hadn't hit a damned thing but broken window and the damned doors. Hours ticked by and Coker wondered where Burns was. He should have circled on Gunn by now.

Langley started toward the door, pistol in hand.

A hat appeared above the top of the batwings, the back of a man's head.

Gunn!

"There he is!" screamed Coker. "Kill him! Kill him, Langley! Shoot him in the back!"

And then the hat was gone.

Outside, a pistol boomed.

CHAPTER NINETEEN

Willa saved Gunn's life. She gave him the precious seconds he needed.

Unwittingly. Lying on the ground between Gunn and Paul Burns she didn't see the latter when he came around the building. She looked up, saw Gunn and started to rise, come toward him.

Gunn backed up to the doors, stepped back in the slight box made by the adobe doorframe. His hand slid behind his back, groped for the pistol shoved next to his backbone. For a second or two, Burns could not get a clear shot.

"Get down, Willa!" he growled low. "Behind you—a man with a gun!"

Willa turned, looked over her shoulder. She saw Burns, then, and threw herself flat.

Gunn went into a crouch, pistol cocked and in his hand. He stepped away from the doors, out of the door frame.

Burns didn't expect it. He had seen Gunn's empty holster. Now Gunn had a pistol in his hand.

Gunn fired.

Burns took the bullet in the center of his chest. His gun arm flew straight up in the air. Blood gushed from his chest. The bullet flattened, mushroomed against his breastbone, broke through, slammed into the spine like a miniature hammerhead. The air rushed from his lungs. Blood gushed up in his throat. Paralysis numbed him as the spinal cord severed. He fell to the ground, feet twitching.

Willa covered her eyes, retched.

Gunn ejected the .45 hull, shoved a fresh bullet in the empty chamber.

"Get out of here, Willa," he said, "quick as you can."

She turned, saw his smoking pistol and scrambled to her feet. She ran across the street toward the hotel, the only haven she knew.

Gunn waited until she reached the doors, then drew back against the wall of the saloon. Burns stopped twitching. The fire inside the cantina died out.

Randy's hand reached the butt of his pistol.

Slicker Langley came around the bar, saw the girls straddling Coker's son. He waded into them, flailed his free arm. The back of his hand caught Esmerelda in the face. She reeled under the impact, fell to one side. Jenny tried to stand up. Langley knocked her down, whacking her high on the head so that she tumbled backwards, rolled a complete somersault.

"Thanks, Slicker," said Randy, rising to his feet. "Where's that fucking Gunn?"

"Outside."

Cantwell stood in front of the batwings.

He heard the shot, wondered if Burns had killed Gunn. He couldn't see a damned thing.

Not at first. Then, he saw Willa running across the

street toward the hotel.

"That gal's a-runnin' away," he called to Coker, over his shoulder.

"Let her go," said Jason. "Randy, you all right?"

Randy shoved past Langley, came around the bar. "Pa, we got to get Gunn."

The burros were now huddled in a far corner of the room, moping, lost. Randy glanced at them and realized what had caused the commotion. Esmerelda and Jenny were held at bay by Langley who stood at the street end of the bar, uncertain what to do. The women were not a danger to him, but they were distracting. Cantwell reloaded his gun.

Outside, Gunn heard the empty shells clicking free of the cylinder. It was time to make his move.

He crouched, slid into the batwing door low. It swung open. Cantwell stared at him wide-eyed, a bullet in his fingers, ready to slip into the cylinder.

"Oh, shit," he said.

"Drop it," warned Gunn.

Cantwell ignored the advice, cocked the pistol. Langley raised his pistol, aimed it at Gunn.

Gunn saw both movements, shot Cantwell. The .45 bucked in his hand. Flame and lead spewed from the barrel. The bullet hit Cantwell in the heart, ripped through a rib, exploded a bone into sharp slivers. The heart burst with the expanded lead ball. Blood gushed from Cantwell's chest as his eyes went blank with shock and surprise. He pulled the trigger of his pistol, but he was already falling. The shot went wild, broke another pane out of the window.

Langley had a poor shot at Gunn, but he fired anyway.

Jason Coker couldn't see enough of Gunn to

shoot. Cantwell was falling as he rose from behind the table.

Langley's shot whizzed over Gunn's head, thunked into the adobe wall next to the door.

Gunn hurled himself headlong at the bar, hit the dirt and rolled to his left. Jason fired both barrels of the Greener. Lead sprayed where Gunn had been a split second before, gouging out grooves in the dirt, spanging out into the street, rattling off the batwings.

Jenny Lee screamed, ran towards the far end of the bar.

Randy Coker grabbed her with one arm, dragged her toward his father.

"Missed him," shouted Jason. "Langley, grab the Lassiter gal, we got to get out."

Jason fumbled for fresh shells. He cracked the double-barreled shotgun, ejecting the empty shells.

Langley turned, unable to see Gunn on the floor, and grabbed Esmerelda. She fought him, kicking and clawing with her hands, but he was too strong for her. He forced her in front of him toward the saloon hallway where the Cokers were backing out.

Gunn crawled to the protection of the bar. He reached it, then stuck his head out, pistol in front of him.

Randy spotted him, fired a round. The bullet tore a four-inch chunk of wood from the bar, showered Gunn's face with splinters.

Gunn fired blindly, hugged the floor.

The burros, frightened at the burst of gunfire, panicked. They shot from their huddle like a covey of flushing quail. One jack raced for the front doors. The jenny stampeded toward Randy Coker while the other jack skidded into a table, overturned it and bucked out of its predicament in a series of leaps over fallen chairs.

Guns boomed. Smoke filled the air. Orange flashes perforated the smoke. The jack heading for the door was struck by a bullet. It stumbled, its hind legs collapsing as its spine disintegrated. It came to rest with a sickening lurch, a few feet from Gunn.

Jason Coker barely eluded the jenny. He stumbled toward the back door, disgusted, fearful of being trapped in that narrow space. Behind him, Randy shoved Jenny, following after his father. Langley was still firing at Gunn, using Esmerelda as a shield.

Gunn threw down on him just as a patch of smoke cleared to give him a clear shot. He squeezed the trigger, felt the Colt respond. He fanned the hammer back, fired again. Both balls found their marks. Langley danced as the bullets hammered into his flesh. The first shot caught him in the left side, the second slammed into his left shoulder, twisting him around. He screamed in pain, tried to regain his stance, but Esmerelda shoved him as she broke free.

"Get her!" said Jason, holding the back door open. "I'll take the Carter gal. Dammit, Randy, get to it. Langley's done for."

Randy pushed Jenny toward the door, ran up to Esmerelda. He grabbed her hair, jerked her backwards. She turned to fight him, but he released his grip on her locks, shifted it to her neck. He held her in a vise grip. Her eyes bulged, her skin turned blue. Randy ringnecked her, then, pulled her backwards.

Jason ran towards a small butte to the south, prodding Jenny with the Greener. Behind them, Randy pulled Esmerelda after him.

Gunn had his hands full. Langley wasn't done for. He was alive, though badly wounded. He crawled to shelter behind the end of the bar, blocking a rush by Gunn for the back door. Every time Gunn tried to fight his way out, Langley squeezed off a round. Gunn heard his own hammer click on a spent cartridge. He cursed, reloaded. Langley reloaded at the same time.

Gunn waited, listening.

"Langley?"

"Yair?"

"Looks like it's just you and me."

"I ain't done for yet, Gunn."

"Coker's left you holding the bag, Langley. The outside man is dead, so is this other feller."

Gunn didn't know their names. Didn't care. He wanted to get past Langley, but he was pinned. If he tried for the door, Langley could blast him to pieces. If he crawled toward him on either side of the bar he would have a gun barrel right down his throat. The Cokers were getting clean away, with Jenny and L.D. as hostages.

"Don't make no never mind to me, Gunn. You hurt me bad, but I'll kill your ass if I can."

Gunn drew a breath, considered the situation. Langley was wounded. That made him doubly dangerous. The man had nothing to lose. Either wound was probably not fatal if he didn't let them go too long without tending to them. But this was no time to wait it out. Every second that went by put Coker and his son further out of reach. Langley wasn't in shock, or didn't seem to be. He was a good shot and he was in a strong position.

Yet, something had to be done. And done quick.

Gunn wondered if he could rush Langley. Get to his feet, start shooting and run a zig-zag pattern. He might take a round or two, but he'd get Langley, maybe. Or Langley might shoot him in the head and he'd go down forever. No, there had to be a better way.

The seconds slid by. The silence shuddered the room to a standstill.

Tom Yire wondered what was happening. There had been no gunfire now for several seconds. Or minutes. It was damned quiet. Paul Burns lay sprawled in the dirt, flies eating at the blood on his chest, flocking to his empty staring eyes.

No sign of Casey, or the others. They were holed up along the street. Didn't know any more than he.

Was Gunn dead? Were they all dead in there? He strained his ears to hear. Nothing.

Macabee showed his face a few doors down.

"Yire? What's going on?"

"I don't know," said Tom. "Beats me."

"Maybe they all died in there."

"No, I don't think so."

"Why?"

"Hell, I don't know. A hunch. It's just too quiet."

Macabee was silent. His head disappeared and Tom turned to look over at the Pozo. It was dark as pitch inside. The sun was climbing high in the sky and the shade in front of the cantina was deep. But he had to know. He came out of his place of concealment in the doorway of the butcher shop. He started walking across the street, pistol held at the ready.

Jason Coker chuckled to himself. They had made it! They had gotten clean away. Their horses were behind the butte, shaded from the morning sun. Just as they had left them. He knocked Jenny to the ground, stood over her, the shotgun pointed at her head ominously. A few seconds later, Randy brought Esmerelda around the rocks.

Esmerelda panted, out of breath. "You can't get away with this," she glared at the two men. Her eyes turned to Jenny, softened with pity. "We'll get out of this."

"Shut up," said Jason.

"What now, Pa? It's going to be hard packin' two women. If they get a posse they'll cut us down."

"Cut some lead rope," Jason told his son.

"You're takin' them?"

"For a ways. Be quick about it. I'll lead one, you take the other. We'll have to leave them untied."

"That Esmerelda's a damned snake. She'll . . ."

"She'll do what I tell her to. Both of them will."

Randy reluctantly cut lead ropes from a lariat on one of the horse's saddle ring. He made them just long enough to give the lead animal room, but not long enough so that either one of the women could get too far from tether.

Jason talked to the women.

"I'm going to cut you loose," he said. "If either of you whines, kicks, runs or screams, I won't waste time with you. I'll shoot you dead. Clear?"

Jenny and Esmerelda looked at Jason. They nodded. Jason's eyes were cold, determined. They knew he meant what he said.

"Fine," he said. "We'll get along fine. You don't mean shit to me. It's Gunn I want and I'll kill any number of ladies to get at him."

Jenny looked at Esmerelda as Jason cut their bonds. Esmerelda returned the look, but one eye closed in a wink.

Gunn knew what he had to do. It might work.

Strategy, he knew, was a heavy weapon of itself.

The man who was bold, and could keep his enemy off-balance would always win. Whether against one man or ten thousand. Move decisively and move in the direction the enemy doesn't expect. Attack him where he is weakest. This is what he learned during the campaigns in the War Between the States and what gained him a reputation for bravery at Missionary Ridge.

He ventured a peek around the bar. His pistol was right in front of him. He squeezed off a shot, then ducked back.

Langley fired twice in quick succession.

The bullets thunked into the bar, splintering the wood. A bullet ricochetted off the dirt and whined under the batwings. There was a tinkle of breaking glass on the other side of the street as the spent bullet struck.

Gunn didn't wait. He moved. Quietly, quickly.

He holstered his pistol, heaved up to the top of the bar. It was charred, still hot from the fire started by the coal-oil bombs. He ignored the searing heat on his palms and slid, lizard-like toward Langley. He inched along, sure of his slide each time he moved. Luckily, he thought, the bar was clear. There was no bottles or glasses to impede his progress. If Langley didn't hear him or wonder where he was, he could make it. Langley was looking for him at the end of the bar. Not on top of it.

And Langley was wounded, pinned down. He couldn't stand up. Or, even if he could, Gunn could shoot him. He drew his pistol again, held the trigger as he cocked it so there wouldn't be a clicking sound.

Slowly, he crawled across the top of the bar toward Slicker Langley.

CHAPTER TWENTY

Tom Yire threw himself in the dirt as soon as gunfire erupted from inside the saloon.

He froze there, dirt smeared on his face, wondering who was still fighting.

Gunn, for one. So, he was alive.

For a long time he thought the fighting might spill into the street, but now he knew that Gunn must be trapped in there, outnumbered. No, there was only one other pistol against him. It had the same tone when it thundered. Gunn and one other. But who? Coker?

Then it was quiet for a long time.

Tom got to his feet, started walking at an angle toward the Pozo. He came close to Burns' dead body, heard the sussurant sawing of flies feeding on flesh.

Was the shooting over?

He reached the wall, hugged it. Slid along it toward the window. Another shot boomed out and then two more, close together.

The hackles on Tom's neck rose as he heard the whining ricochet. His flesh turned to ice as the bullet sizzle-fried the air and crackled against a glass pane in the hotel across the street.

And then it was quiet again.

Langley made a sound. Gunn froze.

Langley groaned, shifted his weight. Gunn heard him from atop the bar, only a few feet now from the end of the bar.

Gunn slid forward, using his elbows to pull him along the bar. He was careful to keep his right foot from edging over the side. Two inches. Stop. Listen. Another two inches. Slow going. Now he could hear Langley breathing. A foot more and he would be right on top of Langley.

"Gunn?" Langley called.

Gunn waited, cursing.

"Coker's coming back," said Langley. "You ain't got a chance."

Gunn could not reply. To do so would reveal his position. But he could not stay silent, either. Langley would figure it out, sooner or later.

"Gunn, you listenin'? I'm bleedin' and need to look at my wounds. You throw your pistol out and I'll throw mine out."

Gunn knew Langley was lying. He could wait no longer. Every second that went by made his position more dangerous. If Langley managed to get to his feet he'd have Gunn at pointblank range.

Gunn elbowed forward. Six inches. He didn't stop there. Forward again. Now he was near the edge.

He tried to imagine Langley's position. Somewhere in a space no more than three feet wide. But once he peered over would Langley be able to get off the first shot? That was the crucial question. And there was no more time to weigh his chances. It was now . . . or never.

Gunn drew his pistol back, edged to his left. He would drop down for firm footing, swing over the edge shooting. Count on surprise and confusion. Hoping one of the bullets would find a crippling or deadly mark.

Gunn summoned up all his strength.

He was ready. He swung his legs over the bar, threw the weight of his upper torso forward.

At that moment, Tom Yire stepped through the batwing doors.

"Gunn?"

Langley stuck his head and pistol around the side of the bar, fired at Tom.

Gunn hit the floor with his boots, lunged around the backside of the bar. As soon as he saw a target, he fired. White smoke spewed from his pistol as flame and lead burst from the barrel.

Langley was sprawled toward the back hallway.

Tom yelled as Langley's bullet smashed into his arm at the elbow. His pistol clumped into the dirt floor and he staggered into a table.

Langley twisted as Gunn's bullet thudded into his calf. He saw a blurred shape, swung his pistol around for a shot at close range. He looked up and saw Gunn's face, his pale blue eyes through the smoke. Eyes like shining pewter. It was the last thing he saw.

Gunn squeezed the trigger, saw Langley's forehead twitch. The bullet hit the outlaw's forehead dead center, knocking sweat globules from the flesh, blowing brain matter and bone out the back of his skull. Langley went into spasmic contortions as his nervous system shattered, collapsed.

Langley twisted grotesquely in the dirt, then lay still. A wreath of smoke hovered over his dead body. Gunn stepped over him, saw Tom, holding onto the table with his good hand, swaying there, in pain. His face was drained of blood.

"Tom? You all right?"

Tom looked at his shattered elbow, crimson with

blood, the shirt torn.

"I'll make it," he said tightly.

"Both Cokers are alive. They have Esmerelda and Jenny. Went out back. I've got to get after them."

Gunn was already shoving a fresh shell in the cylinder of his Colt.

"Yeah. Go. Don't worry about me."

Gunn hit the back door in long strides, unmindful of the pain in his leg. At least it wasn't stiff anymore. His head was clear now. Langley had held him at bay and he was out of the way for good. The question now was where had Coker gone? He had horses, Gunn did not. A quick tracking and he might have to return, saddle up Esquire. Coker held the aces now and a couple of high kickers. Jenny and Esmerelda.

The sunlight was blinding. Gunn squinted, saw the tracks, clear in the dirt. He looked beyond, saw the butte, made a mental calculation. That was the nearest cover. It had to be where Coker had hid his horses. His eyes scanned the broken rocky landscape for sign. For dust. For anything moving or out of place among the saguaro, the coetus, mesquite.

Nothing.

He broke out for the butte in a dead run, pistol in hand. The pain in his leg throbbed and he felt a hot dampness seeping onto his flesh beneath the bandage.

Across the street, Willa listened to the gunfire. Gretchen held on to her. Both girls shook with fear.

"Kill them, Gunn, kill them!" hissed the billowy Gretchen.

Willa looked at Gretchen.

"You care, don't you?"

"Yes."

"About Gunn?"

"Yes. Very much." Gretchen tried to hide her face, but Willa chucked her under the chin.

"Did you . . . did he . . . ?"

"Willa . . ."

"Gretchen! You devil you!"

The shooting died down. It was quiet.

"Willa, it was just something that happened. He was hurt and I . . ."

"You don't have to explain. I'm worried about Jenny Lee now. And Esmerelda, much as I dislike her. They need our help more than Gunn right now."

"Where are they?"

"If they're not dead, I know where they'll be. Can you get a couple of pistols? We'll go after them."

"I know where Tom keeps some. Behind the bar in the Elk's Head."

"Get them!"

Gretchen went through the hotel lobby into the saloon. Willa stood at the window watching the Pozo as Tom reeled out.

"Gunn's alive!" he shouted. "He's gone after Coker!"

Gretchen returned, breathless, moments later. She handed Willa a loaded pistol. She carried one herself. They were both small Colt pocket pistols, .31 caliber.

"Come on," said Willa. "We haven't a moment to lose."

The two women burst from the hotel, running. They raced by Tom who held his shattered arm high, squeezing it above the elbow to staunch the bleeding.

"Hey!" he yelled. But the women were gone past him, darting between buildings. Men stepped tentatively outside their hiding places and started toward him. In a moment he was surrounded, telling his story of how he got wounded, how he had seen

Gunn kill Slicker Langley.

Randy finished tying the lead ropes to the women's horses. He handed one to his father.

"All right. Get 'em mounted up, Randy."

Esmerelda shot Jenny Lee a look.

Randy walked toward them, swaggering.

"You heard him," he gruffed. "Get up, Esmerelda. Jenny, you take that other horse."

Neither woman moved.

Angered, Randy stepped close, drew back his hand to strike Esmerelda. She didn't flinch. As he hurled his open hand to slap her, she took a step forward, grabbed his other arm and jerked him off balance. Randy's swing missed, his hand passing just over Esmerelda's head.

Esmerelda sank her teeth in Randy's wrist.

He howled in pain. Jenny leaped into the fray, kicking high. Her toe caught Randy in the groin. He howled again, the pain in two locations as Esmerelda gripped him with her teeth, biting down as hard as she could.

"What the hell . . ." Jason saw his son being attacked by the two women, but the seriousness of the situation did not strike him all at once. He strode to Randy, grabbed his shoulder to pull him away from the attacking women.

Jenny grabbed Randy's other arm, pulled on it. Now Randy was being jerked in two directions.

"Turn loose of my son!" ordered Jason.

"Get 'em off me, Pa!"

Jenny jerked Randy around. Esmerelda's teeth lost their grip, but she was not about to give up. She waded into Randy, flailing her fists.

"Raper!" she screamed.

Jason raised his shotgun, fired a shell into the air.

Jenny let loose of Randy's arm, frightened.

Esmerelda whacked Randy in the eye. He screamed, doubled over.

"Goddamned little bitches!" said Jason. "Get away from him or I'll let you have the other barrel."

Esmerelda glared at him. Jenny backed away as the shotgun came level.

Randy staggered in a circle, holding onto his wrist. One eye was full of tears.

Both women stood there, panting from exertion, defiant, now that Randy was hurt. They were standing far enough apart so that Jason could only shoot one of them. Jason started to correct this, when they all heard running footsteps.

Gunn heard the shotgun blast go off and his heart sank. Behind him he saw Willa and Gretchen running after him, wielding small pistols. He tried to wave them back, but they ignored him. Now the butte loomed up. He drew his pistol.

He heard shouts.

A moment later as Gunn halted his rush, he saw Randy peer from behind the butte.

"It's Gunn!" Randy yelled. He was rubbing one eye, clawing for his pistol.

"Get him!" came a shout from Jason. Gunn could not see the man.

Randy drew his pistol, fired. Gunn hammered back, fired, and threw himself in the dirt, headlong. Randy fired again. A dust spout kicked up inches from Gunn's face.

Where was Jason Coker?

Out of the corner of his eye, Gunn saw Willa and Gretchen veer to the left. The foolish women! They were going to circle the butte from the other side!

Gunn had his hands full with Randy. Randy raced

to a saguaro, using it for cover. He fired again. Sand stung Gunn's face as the bullet plowed into the earth, two feet in front of him. He rolled, cracked off another shot. He saw the cactus twitch, a chunk of it fly off aimlessly. Too high!

"Gunn! Coker's loading his shotgun! Look out!"

Jenny's voice. Gunn fired twice more. Four shots gone.

Gunn knew he had to get out of his pinned-down position. Coker might just shoot the women, all four of them, and back up Randy. He'd be outnumbered badly if that happened.

"Randy!" Gunn shouted. "You got me."

"Huh?" said Randy.

Gunn waited for Randy to take a look. He was ready.

Randy's face appeared from behind the saguaro.

Gunn steadied, aimed at a point on the tip of the youth's chin. He squeezed off the shot. Randy's face blew away. His body twisted, lurched, then fell with a thump.

"Randy?" Coker calling as the silence built up.

Gunn was already up and running. He rounded the butte, saw why Jason had not come to his son's aid. Gretchen and Willa had him covered with the pocket pistols. Jenny and Esmerelda were covered by Jason's shotgun.

It was a standoff!

Jason glared at Gunn. Gunn saw that both hammers were cocked on the Greener.

"You still load your handgun with five shots, Gunn?" Coker mocked. " 'Member you used to do that."

Gunn said nothing. His pale eyes did not flicker. His pistol held steady on Coker's midsection. The weapon was cocked, the hammer back like a snake about to strike.

"Yeah, you put your burying money in that sixth cylinder as I recall. And you already shot five times. I counted. But you may have six bullets in the Colt. You'll get one off, no more. I pull both triggers at once and two women die right fast."

"You win, Coker," said Gunn.

"No! You can't!" shrieked Esmerelda.

But Gunn had already dropped the hammer on the Colt, had it by the barrel, butt facing Coker. Gunn's finger was just barely in the trigger guard. He stepped towards Coker.

"Empty, huh?" Coker grinned as he reached for the butt of the pistol. "I figgered as much."

Surprise lit Coker's features as Gunn performed a "border shift." He twirled the Colt, stopped its spin by thumbing the hammer back. Gunn's finger pulled the trigger, hard. No finesse, just a shot at close range. The bullet caught Coker in the belly. He lurched. Gunn grabbed the barrel of the Greener, jerked it out of Coker's hands.

Coker staggered, clawed for his sidearm.

Gunn tossed the shotgun down.

Coker drew. Gunn opened the gate to the cylinder, but he knew it would be too late.

Twin reports broke the deadly silence.

Coker twitched as two .31 caliber balls ripped into his back and side. Willa and Gretchen fired again. Coker danced over to the butte wall, fell, his head crashing into the rock. He turned, stared dumbly up into the sky. His mouth moved, but no sound came out. He gave a short gasp and his head fell forward.

Gunn drew a breath, reloaded his pistol, holstered it.

"Thanks, Willa, Gretchen." Gunn hugged them both. Then he turned to Jenny and Esmerelda. "You both held on. I'm grateful to all of you.'' He hugged each of them.

Tom Yire and the townspeople came up. Tom's arm was in a sling.

''Need any help?'' he asked.

The women surrounded Gunn, embraced and kissed him in turn.

Gunn grinned.

''No, don't need a thing,'' said Gunn, tilting his hat back on his head. ''Maybe a nice big quiet room in the hotel. For about a day.''

''You can have anything you want in this town,'' said Casey, stepping forward. ''I never saw anything like it.''

''You got some fine women here,'' said Gunn. ''They did Coker in. Kind of what was meant to be.''

Jenny snuggled next to Gunn.

''You mean . . .'' she ventured.

''I mean,'' he said, ''that Coker was responsible for killing my wife. A long time ago. He broke out of jail for what? To meet his end at the hands of women. All four of you. That's what he was after, I guess. What I was after when I put him in jail in the first place . . .''

''What's that?'' asked Esmerelda, an arm around Gunn's waist.

''Justice,'' said Gunn. ''Justice.''